PENGUIN

FAUST, PART I

JOHANN WOLFGANG VON GOETHE was born in Frankfurt-am-Main in 1749. He studied in Leipzig, where he showed interest in the occult, and in Strasbourg, where Herder introduced him to Shakespeare's works and to folk poetry. He produced some essays and lyrical verse, and at twenty-four wrote *Goetz von Berlichingen*, a play which brought him national fame and established him in the current *Sturm und Drang* movement. *Werther*, a tragic romance, was an even greater success. Goethe began work on *Faust*, and *Egmont*, another tragedy, before being invited to join the government at Weimar. His interest in the classical world led him to leave suddenly for Italy in 1786, and the *Italian Journey* recounts his travels there. *Iphigenie auf Tauris* and *Torquato Tasso*, classical dramas, were begun at this time. Returning to Weimar, Goethe started the second part of *Faust*, encouraged by Schiller. During this late period he finished the series of *Wilhelm Meister* books and wrote many other works, including *The West-Eastern Divan* and *Elective Affinities*. He also directed the State Theatre and worked on scientific theories in evolutionary botany, anatomy and colour. Goethe was married in 1806. He finished *Faust* before he died in 1832.

DAVID CONSTANTINE was born in 1944 in Salford, Lancashire. He read modern languages at Wadham College, Oxford; he wrote a D.Phil. there on the poetry of Friedrich Hölderlin. From 1969 to 1981 he was Lecturer then Senior Lecturer in German at the University of Durham, and from 1981 to 2000 was Fellow in German at the Queen's College, Oxford. He is now visiting Professor in the School of English, University of Liverpool. From January to May 2004 he was Distinguished Visiting Professor in the Department of German, University of Rutgers, New Jersey. He lives in Oxford, working as a freelance writer and translator. He has published half a dozen volumes of poetry, most recently *Collected Poems*, all with Bloodaxe Books. He is a translator of Hölderlin, Goethe, Kleist and Brecht. He was the literary editor of *Oxford Magazine* and is now joint editor (with Helen Constantine) of *Modern Poetry in Translation*.

A. S. BYATT was born in 1936 and educated in York and at Newnham College, Cambridge, of which she is now an Honorary Fellow. She taught English at University College, London, from 1972 to 1983. She appears regularly on radio and television, and writes academic articles and literary journalism both in England and abroad. Her fiction includes *The Shadow of the Sun*; *The Game*; *The Virgin in the Garden*; *Still Life*; *Sugar and Other Stories*; *Possession*, winner of the 1990 Booker Prize and the 1990 *Irish Times*/Aer Lingus International Fiction Prize; the novella *Angels and Insects*; *The Matisse Stories*; *The Djinn in the Nightingale's Eye*, a collection of fairy stories; *Babel Tower*; *Elementals: Stories of Fire and Ice*; *The Biographer's Tale*; *A Whistling Woman* and *The Little Black Book of Stories*. Her work has been translated into 28 languages. Her critical work includes *Degrees of Freedom: The Early Novels of Iris Murdoch*, *Unruly Times* (on Wordsworth and Coleridge) and, with the psychoanalyst Ignês Sodré, *Imagining Characters: Six Conversations About Women Writers*. *Passions of the Mind*, a collection of critical essays, appeared in 1991; a new collection, *On Histories and Stories*, appeared in 2000; *Portraits in Fiction*, a study of the relationship between painting and the novel, and (ed.) *Selected Essays, Poems and Other Writings*, by George Eliot, in 2001. She was appointed DBE in 1999.

JOHANN WOLFGANG VON GOETHE

Faust

The First Part of the Tragedy

Translated with an Introduction and Notes by
DAVID CONSTANTINE
with a Preface by A. S. BYATT

PENGUIN BOOKS

PENGUIN CLASSICS

Published by the Penguin Group
Penguin Books Ltd, 80 Strand, London WC2R ORL, England
Penguin Group (USA) Inc., 375 Hudson Street, New York, New York 10014, USA
Penguin Group (Canada), 10 Alcorn Avenue, Toronto, Ontario, Canada M4V 3B2
(a division of Pearson Penguin Canada Inc.)
Penguin Ireland, 25 St Stephen's Green, Dublin 2, Ireland
(a division of Penguin Books Ltd)
Penguin Group (Australia), 250 Camberwell Road, Camberwell, Victoria 3124, Australia
(a division of Pearson Australia Group Pty Ltd)
Penguin Books India Pvt Ltd, 11 Community Centre, Panchsheel Park, New Delhi – 110 017, India
Penguin Group (NZ), cnr Airborne and Rosedale Roads, Albany, Auckland 1310, New Zealand
(a division of Pearson New Zealand Ltd)
Penguin Books (South Africa) (Pty) Ltd, 24 Sturdee Avenue, Rosebank 2196, South Africa

Penguin Books Ltd, Registered Offices: 80 Strand, London WC2R ORL, England

www.penguin.com

First published 1808
This translation first published in Penguin Classics 2005
2

Translation and editorial material copyright © David Constantine, 2005
Preface copyright © A. S. Byatt, 2005
All rights reserved

The moral right of the translator has been asserted

Set in 10.25/12.25 pt PostScript Adobe Sabon
Typeset by Rowland Phototypesetting Ltd, Bury St Edmunds, Suffolk
Printed in England by Clays Ltd, St Ives plc

Contents

Preface

Faust is one of the magnetic figures in Western culture. We use his fate to plot our thoughts about human nature and destiny, along with Don Juan, Hamlet, Don Quixote, Peer Gynt, Captain Ahab, Wagner's Wotan, Balzac's Vautrin and Ulysses. These are all male figures who are what Marlowe called 'overweeners'. They are clever and passionate, their intellects are restless, they want too much (whatever that is). They resist apparent order – the two 'good' men in the list, Quixote and Hamlet, see more things in heaven and earth than the common man, and are destroyed partly by their own imaginations. Most of the rest make pacts with dubious or evil forces, from Satan to modern capitalism, and are corrupted and destroyed. They ally themselves with tricksters, manipulators and demons. They take on aspects of each other's tales – Faust mixes with Don Juan; Peer Gynt is trickster, entrepreneur and fool; Vautrin is Satan, Faust and Mephistopheles.

Faust and Mephistopheles are also part of a string of paired characters – master and servant, wise man and fool, man and demon – whose dialogue represents (in part) the struggle in one mind between scepticism and idealism, self-seeking and altruism, honour and cynicism. Falstaff is Prince Henry's comic demon, descended from the Vice in the mystery plays. Diderot's amoral Jacques le Fataliste is both a servant and the voice of nihilism. Kafka brilliantly reversed the relationship by writing a parable in which Don Quixote is Sancho Panza's demon, who is deflected from destroying the 'free and responsible' Sancho by a diet of chivalric fantasy, leading to a comic madness which 'harmed nobody'. In literary dialogues between man and devil, from Marlowe to Thomas Mann and Mikhail Bulgakov, the devil has the best lines, and most of the human wit. This goes deeper than the simple dramatization of seductive charms, designed to defraud and betray. Dramatized devils represent human scepticism that moralists and idealists dare not admit. They also represent the terror of death, annihilation and inhuman eternity, which they understand better than their prey. When these two force-fields are combined, there are new possibilities both of horror and bitter comedy. In Adelbert von Chamisso's *An Attempt* (1804), a Faust published after Goethe's *Faust. A Fragment*, the evil spirit induces despair in his Faust with the Kantian idea that we cannot know reality. The Faust story comes from a Christian world in which the Lord forbade the eating of the Tree of Knowledge of Good and Evil, and the Devil takes the souls of those who sin through the intellect or the senses. It is still potent in a world where human beings have become afraid, both of what human ingenuity can achieve, and of the limited ability of human mind and moral orders to control those achievements responsibly.

Goethe's *Faust* came after a vast number of popular and literary Fausts, and in turn gave rise to a whole new literature of poetry and drama.[1] Marlowe's Faust, though written by an atheist, derives its power and terror from the reality of the eternal damnation, which tortures both man and witty demon, against which the drama is played out. The Faust figure goes back to the conjuring magus who really tried to control spirits, and to times when men and women were burned for witchcraft and blasphemy. The religious Faust comes from a world in which Luther saw the devil and threw his inkpot at him. Goethe first met Faust, as a child, in the puppet plays, 'which resounded and hummed within me in many tonal variations.'[2] The puppet plays combine slapstick farce with magical illusions and conjuring in both senses. It is not insignificant that one of the greatest puppeteers, Georg Geisselbrecht, at the beginning of the nineteenth century, finally gave up playing Faust, out of some fear of the conjuration of devils and the opening of the Pit. He feared for his own soul.[3]

Goethe's *Faust* begins by using this Nordic and medieval

Gothic material, with its Germanic background of dusty study, church and university, the essential nature of which, as all critics have observed, is at odds with his own anti-Christian, rational, optimistic world-view. In what becomes *Faust, Part I*, he introduces the tragic story of Gretchen, which is not part of the older versions. He also – at the end of *Part II* – saves Faust, tricking Mephistopheles of the fulfilment of his pact, or wager, through the intervention of some seductive boy cherubs. A saved Faust deprives the original tale of much of its energy and power. *Part II* represents, as Schiller said, a story which 'runs, and must run, into the crass and shapeless'.[4] In this giddy phantasmagoria Faust and Mephisto make paper money for emperors, attend a classical Walpurgis Night, call up a phantom Helen of Troy, and then bring her back in solid flesh from Hades to bear Faust's child, Euphorion, doomed and Byronic. Faust wins battles and rolls back the sea to make new land. At the age of one hundred, blinded and accompanied by Care, he finally asks the fleeting moment to stay, but is carried away by a heavenly choir. *Part II* represents the other side, not only of Goethe, but of German art and thought – a dialogue with ancient classicism and non-Christian mythologies.

Schiller wrote that 'We can never lose sight of the contradictory double nature of humankind and the failed endeavour to unite the divine and the physical in the human being',[5] and saw the work as a philosophical poem. If anything holds the whole of the two parts of *Faust* together it is the power and *diversity* of the poetry, the range of forms used, from medieval ballad to classical trimeter. That is one paradox. The other is that it is held together by Goethe himself – it is not an autobiography, but is one of those great works of literature into which a writer has been able to combine his ranging preoccupations and understanding as he worked. Karl Eibl's brilliant book on *Faust* has the splendid title *Das Monumentale Ich* – 'The Monumental "I"'. But the work isn't self-regarding or an apologia for the self. It is a man thinking and making images in extraordinary language. It is the work of a thinker interested in government and theatre, astrology and alchemy, geology, morphology, colour forms, charlatanism, sex of all kinds, and the stuff of life, mind and culture. Goethe is amazing. Faust himself, in Goethe's version, is frequently both tedious and curiously non-existent, the puppet of the plot, of the God of the prologue, of Mephistopheles and of Goethe himself.

A. C. Bradley remarked that after Hamlet Shakespeare never again attempted to make an intelligent tragic hero. Hamlet is a thinker who cannot bring himself to act. His utterance of his inner life in his soliloquies is the intense point of his drama, which is so long because it nevertheless does contain action and tragedy. Shakespeare's other tragic heroes are soldiers and men of action, trapped by events and other people and their own weaknesses. Faust's traditional sin is 'curiosity' – the desire for knowledge, including the knowledge of good and evil, Adam's sin. The Faust story is the tale of the damnation of thinking men. It is an irony that Goethe's thinking Faust thinks best at the beginning, when he rewrites the opening of the Gospel of St John – 'In the beginning was the Word', as 'In the beginning was the Deed' (1224, 1237), for this Faust does very little except talk, and the action of the drama (apart from Gretchen's tragedy) is not dramatic. It is diffuse and symbolic. It is a commonplace of dramatic criticism that the Romantic poets wrote bad plays because the kind of things they wanted to say were best conveyed in monologues, or dramatic monologues – the true conflict was between parts of an argument, or a world-view, or a psychic tension. It is, so to speak, theatre in the head. Wordsworth and Coleridge, Tennyson and Browning wrote plays in which people described their feelings, rather than acting and being acted upon. Faust is drama in the head in the sense that it appeals most to one reader, staging its scenes and savouring its words inside his or her own head. There have been triumphant stage productions, but it is a daunting project. Nevertheless, it does not resemble British Romantic verse drama, because its author was interested in, and involved with, theatres. He was Director of the Weimar Court Theatre, and the theatrical, earthly Prelude to Faust displays a comic wisdom about the conflicting priorities of poet, director, comic actor and audience.

In Goethe's novel Wilhelm Meister's Theatrical Mission (an

early version of *Wilhelm Meister's Apprentice Years*), Wilhelm
Meister sets out to use the theatre as a means of moral and
social cultivation, possibly as a way to give the Germans a
unified cultural life. There is room on the stage for those whose
days are normally spent getting and spending to present them-
selves as thinking and passionate beings – to 'appear' and to
'be'.[6] *Faust* had some of its origins in Goethe's interest in the
staged illusions of Mozart's *Magic Flute*. The young Goethe
was interested in puppets and marionettes. Part of the peculiar
quality of the form of the two parts of *Faust* is the way they
transmogrify and shape-shift, operating at all levels, from the
magic lantern and conjuring trick (Mephistopheles in Auer-
bach's tavern, Mephistopheles conjuring up the forms of Helen
and Paris as a court entertainment, the phantasmagoria, both
verbal and visual, of both Walpurgis Nights) to the tortured
inner debate of Faust's first speeches, the dramatic directness
of Gretchen and her world, and the cosmological anxieties and
yearnings of the bottled homunculus made by Wagner in
Part II. The work isn't psychic allegory partly because it is so
much about illusion and showmanship.

I agree with those critics, including David Constantine in his
Introduction, who see *Faust* as not ultimately unified or coher-
ent as a work. It flies apart, it pulls apart, it starts too many
flights, and does not end them, or cohere. But one of the ways
in which to think about the kind of unity it does have is to
think about the women in it, Gretchen in *Part I* and Helen in
Part II, and the patterns of language and action in which they
are constructed. Their opposition is a kind of unity. And they
are both part of an idea of the female, *das Ewig-Weibliche*,
which underlies the work, representing both human origins and
the object of desire.

Helen of Troy, phantom or revenant, is a more ancient and
more essential figure from the old Faust legend than the late-
comer, Gretchen. She is the beautiful human body as power –
'Is this the face that launched a thousand ships/ And burned
the topless towers of Ilium?' She is Platonic Beauty, desired
alongside wisdom and knowledge. She is, as the object of
bodily, sexual desire, the ultimate attainment, to die for, to lose

one's soul for. In Greek mythology she is given to Paris by Aphrodite, in reward for the Apple of Discord. In Greek legend and myth she already shows a propensity to appear as a wraith, or a simulacrum – according to one version the 'real' Helen spent the long years of the Trojan War in Egypt, whilst Paris slept with an eidolon, a puppet. In the old Faust legends and plays she sometimes gives Faust a son, Justus Faustus. She is the perfect Face Faust sees in the Witch's Kitchen, for whose sake he is rejuvenated by magic. In *Part II* of Goethe's *Faust* she is conjured twice, once for the Emperor, and once when Mephistopheles, disguised as Phorkyas, a female Fate in the form of a hag with one eye and one fang, brings her and her chorus of handmaids back from the Underworld to be rescued by Faust and to join him in a medieval German castle. The first conjuring, for the Emperor, is Mephistophelean trickery – the figures disappear when desired and touched. The second brings with it Greek tragedy – Helen, confused and distraught, supposes she is returning to Menelaus' house, where she is to prepare for her own sacrifice. Faust 'rescues' her with magic. As a woman this Helen is wonderfully human and real, a beautiful woman and a princess, aware of the unsought effects of her excess of beauty. She bears Faust a son, Euphorion, who hubristically tries to fly like Phaethon and destroys himself – at which point she again becomes a wraith and returns to Hades, leaving only her clothing. The Greek tragedy is gripping; Faust's (successful) attempts to teach her to speak medieval rhyming verse are funny and moving; Euphorion is ludicrous and dramatically bathetic, and the whole episode is a thorough attempt to see and hear the classical world that is vanished – which ends in a sense of its vanishing.

The Gretchen of *Part I*, on the contrary, is a Christian character in a Christian story, taking place in a world where salvation and damnation are real, more real than human acts. It is not a love story. Faust's inclination for the innocent girl is casual and lustful. She is seduced by jewels and fine manners and a kiss. Her innocent fault leads to the death of her mother and brother, and to her brother's curse. It leads also to infanticide, and condemnation by cruel human law to a theatrical execution.

The events are terrible, but the power of Goethe's rendering is in the simplicity of the language. Gretchen would not be Gretchen without the songs she sings, the rhythms she thinks in, and the quite different rhythms of the Church Faust causes her to doubt and disobey. Her first wonderful song, 'There was a king in Thule' (2759), combines the idea of some Nordic extreme with the powerfully simple idea of a love longer and deeper than life, with the 'holy' golden goblet hurled into the water. It is the essence of the ballad and of the values that went with it. The shuttling, hurrying repetitive rhythm of 'Meine Ruh ist hin'[7] both reinforces and destabilizes the world of poetic simplicity. And the sinful Gretchen, in the scene before the Mater Dolorosa and in the cathedral with the Evil Spirit, faces the full blast of the Christian terror that never catches up with this Faust. She sees the Queen of Heaven with a sword in her heart, contemplating her dead Son. In the cathedral she is taunted by the Evil Spirit with the image of the gaping grave and the flames of hell, to the terrible music of the Dies Irae, the Day of Wrath, a measured apocalyptic vision that drowns her small voice and her consciousness. What follows for Gretchen is child murder and madness. She is the human opposite of the Virgin Mary with her dead Son, though she asks to be buried with her slaughtered child on her breast, and Goethe has made it clear that she is naturally motherly, with her tales of caring for her little sister who died. Goethe in Italy rejected the suffering visions of painted martyrdoms. Gretchen lives and dies in a world that believes in them.

The two Walpurgis Nights are tours de force of wild rhythms, orchestrated appearances and disappearances of real, unreal, imagined and shape-shifting creatures, human, inhuman and the two combined. Both at one level represent the flux of chaos out of which forms come to be – and both have their own sexual atmosphere, one derived from medieval witchcraft and wickedness, one from serene classical voluptuousness – which makes Mephistopheles, a creature of the Christian cosmos, socially and morally anxious. Goethe at one point intended to end the Witches' Sabbath with the sexual embrace of witches and goat-formed Satan. The classical Walpurgis Night is inhabited by sphinxes, sirens and many other innocent, earthy and watery creatures, including the wise centaur, Chiron. The dramatic placing of the scene on the Brocken in the Harz Mountains in *Faust, Part I* is crucial to our feeling for the play. It comes between the killing of Valentine and the discovery of Gretchen's crime and fate, and is the one place in the drama where we feel that Faust is carried away and truly tempted by the forces of darkness – most of all by their speed and rush and variety.

At the end of his time on the Brocken Faust sees a pale, heavy-footed child who resembles Gretchen. Mephistopheles makes busy efforts to distract him, telling him that what he sees is 'a magic image, an idol, not alive' (4190) – something he adds angrily, that will turn men to stone, like the Medusa. Faust continues to stare at the dead eyes, the breast, and finally the red ribbon – no wider than a knifeblade – round her neck (like the ribbons flaunted by the aristos in the French Terror). Mephisto continues to hector – 'Fool easily misled, that is the magic art' (4199). This vision of a damned ghost of the not-yet dead is the nearest Goethe's Faust comes either to damnation or repentance. It does also bear some resemblance to the eidolon of Helen, the vanishing wraith. Between this scene and the dramatic horror of Gretchen's dungeon comes a very theatrical Intermezzo, a dream of the Golden Wedding of Oberon and Titania, including a stage manager, a dancing master, Puck, Ariel and a Will-o'-the-Wisp. Unreal stuff, formal unreal stuff, which has an odd effect on our apprehension of the unreal stuff of ghosts, spectres, apparitions and Medusas. 'Glamour' in English is a word for fairy illusion covering a bleak reality. Goethe understands glamour. It is Ariel who leads the choir of spirits who soothe Faust's consciousness at the opening of *Part II* after the tragedy.

Gretchen kills Faust's child. His child by Helen destroys his life with her, by overweening. I think there is a third child, the magical homunculus made of fire and earth in a flask by Wagner, Faust's servant (though he was earlier projected to be made by Faust himself). The homunculus, who does not issue from the union of man and woman, is wise and funny, and vanishes when he breaks his glass and is dissolved in the sea surrounding the chariot of the beautiful Galatea – thus joining earth and fire to air and water. I think the homunculus is in part a theatrical image for the work of art itself – not a Black Art, not a deception, but a forming of something human in miniature which holds together for a time and then is reabsorbed into the primeval flux. His death is a birth, whereas Gretchen's child, and Helen's, are born to die. The fact that Faust does not make the delightful homunculus adds to our sense that he doesn't do anything, is only acted upon. Wagner made the little creature with Faust's original materials and in his old study.

Helen, Gretchen, the witches of the kitchen and the Brocken come together in the concept of the Eternal Female, who appears as the Mater Gloriosa at the end of *Part II*, amongst a singing choir of angels, anchorites and repentant women sinners, including one 'once called Gretchen' (12069) who pleads for Faust. Nobody much likes this scene, which hovers on the rim of the absurd. The best we can do is to connect it to the earlier mysterious scene where Faust has to travel under the earth to the Mothers in order to find the key which will help him release Helen. Faust is terrified of the idea, of the word itself. Mephistopheles describes them deep down (or high up, it is all the same), making and unmaking the images of all creatures. 'They do not see you, they see only patterns' (6290). The final Chorus Mysticus in *Part II* tells us that all that passes is only a semblance, that what is incomplete here becomes actual, that what cannot be described is here enacted – as the Eternal Female draws us onwards. Women, the female, give birth to forms from formlessness, they make shadows – including the shadows and actors of Prospero's speech, who vanish into thin air – into real acts and real things. This in turn takes us back to Faust questioning the nature of reality and illusion in his study at the beginning of *Part I*.

What do modern readers – especially non-Germans – make of *Faust* today? It has always been a difficult play for the English – though it was popular amongst American transcendentalists.

Even those who responded to Gretchen's tragedy in *Part I* have been baffled and sometimes repelled by the exuberance, shocking shifts of tone, learned references and Protean ungraspability of *Part II*. Nobody much likes Faust himself, and very few think his belief in 'striving' ought to have been sufficient to save him. Goethe's failure to punish him for the death of Gretchen – indeed his failure to punish him for anything – leaves readers with a primitive dissatisfaction, to put it mildly.

Two fairly recent accounts of *Faust* today are illuminating in different ways, and seem at first sight to be contradictory. Harold Bloom, in *The Western Canon*, calls Faust 'the most grotesque and unassimilable of major Western poems in dramatic form'. He asks, 'What makes so strange a poem permanent and universal?', and answers himself that it is the 'mythopoeic' counterpoint of *Faust, Part II* which he compares to, and sets above, Blake's Prophetic Books, and includes in his canon. At the beginning of his provocative and exciting essay he says that 'Of all the strongest Western writers, Goethe now seems the least available to our sensibility.' He goes on to make the wise point that, 'though he stands at the true beginning of imaginative literature in German, Goethe is, from a Western perspective, an end rather than a beginning.'[8] He sees a direct line from Homer to Goethe; literature changes with the advent of the modern world. In some sense Goethe's power sums up both the classical and the Christian traditions before the French Revolution. He is not part of our world.

Franco Moretti, on the other hand, sees *Faust* as part of a new genre which he calls 'Modern Epic', a category containing indisputably great and important books which nevertheless have rebarbative and difficult aspects, are hard to read and describe, and are sometimes incomplete, put together by *bricoleurs* (as described by Claude Lévi-Strauss). These works include *Moby-Dick*, *Ulysses*, Ezra Pound's *Cantos*, Gabriel García Márquez's *One Hundred Years of Solitude*. They are books with pantechnicon forms, that grow by accretion or collecting. Goethe, Moretti maintains, began by choosing Faust as a tragic hero, and went on to realize that Mephistopheles was the principal character in a new, ironic, protean form. Bloom's version and Moretti's are not mutually exclusive – they both recognize something dynamic and unachieved and excessive in the text. For an Anglo-Saxon reader to have any real sense of what the work is, it must be translated into *good* poetry. This is one of the most daunting challenges to any translator, and David Constantine has met it with the requisite energy and plainness, subtlety, lyricism and wit.

Man and demon continued their conversation after Goethe. German poets and playwrights produced many more Fausts. The operas by Charles Gounod, Arrigo Boito and Hector Berlioz were followed by *Faust, a Rock Opera*. Goethe's *Faust* was the beginning of Russian interest in the story, and was translated by, among others, Boris Pasternak. I think of two Russian texts when I think of the afterlife of *Faust* – the terrifying and brilliant dialogue between Ivan Karamazov and the Devil in *The Brothers Karamazov*, and Mikhail Bulgakov's phantasmagoric and furiously energetic masterpiece, *The Master and Margarita* (finished in 1938).

In Bulgakov's novel, Voland (one of the names of the Faustian Mephisto) and accompanying demons and black cat rampage through Moscow, in scenes that include an infernal ball and a theatrical conjuring with paper money and vanishing goods. Margarita (Gretchen, Margarethe) becomes a witch and, among other acts, prays for the remission of the punishment of a child-murdering girl. The epigraph to the novel is Mephisto's self-description from *Faust*:

FAUST
   So then, who are you?
MEPHISTO
                    A part of the power who
   Wills evil always but always works the good.

This Voland suggests that the existence of Evil is an inescapable part of the existence of Good. 'What would your good do if evil did not exist, and what would the earth look like if shadows disappeared from it?'

The devil who visits Ivan Karamazov also quotes Goethe. Ivan is a Faust figure in that he is intellectually arrogant and questions both the divine and the human order. He believes and doesn't believe that his devil is a part of himself, a hallucination split off and visible. The devil appears as a sordid and vulgar 'lackey' or 'flunkey', and is both ingratiating and morally riddling. 'But, dear Lord, I don't claim to be your equal in intellect. Mephistopheles, when he appeared to Faust, introduced himself as one who desired evil but did only good. Well, that's as he pleases, but I'm quite the opposite. I'm perhaps the only man in the universe who loves truth and sincerely desires good.'[9] This devil desires to save Ivan's soul in order to claim it, and mocks Ivan's idea that humanity will be innocent and blessed once the idea of God is destroyed. Ivan is the author of the story of the Grand Inquisitor, and his devil further mocks him by claiming that his art – his iconoclastic passionate stories – is the devil's own work. This devil is the continuing presence of the religious sense – however equivocal and tricksy – in the consciousness of a rational atheist.

The German Faust is re-embodied in Thomas Mann's great and witty and appalling *Doctor Faustus* (1947). This is, as Erich Heller observed, in one sense an 'unwriting' of Goethe's Faust.[10] It is the story of another curious overweener, Adrian Leverkühn ('to live audaciously'), whose pact with the devil makes him able to compose great music, but condemns him to die, like Nietzsche who is one of his models, in a syphilitic disintegration and mindlessness. Leverkühn also resembles Ivan Karamazov, and holds a long dialogue which is a parody of Ivan's with that other sleazy, casuistical devil. This devil has the quality, reminiscent of Dante's Lucifer, of creating an absolutely icy atmosphere around him. He is freezing to resist the flames, he says. Leverkühn's story is more a parody of the *Faustbuch* (first published in 1587) than of Goethe, and ends with his collapse into madness before a gathering of friends, where he announces to them that he is eternally damned. The music he writes is both German and Faustian, moving from lyrics through the oratorio for puppets, based on the *Gesta Romanorum*, and the 'Apocalypse with Figures', based on

Dürer's woodcuts of the Last Judgement, to his final triumph, 'The Lamentation of Dr Faustus'. The narrator of the 'biography', Serenus Zeitblom, a liberal humanist, begins his tale on 27 May 1943 (the day Thomas Mann began to write the novel) and records the fall of the corrupt and 'Satanic' Nazi empire in comments interpolated through his account of the collapse of Leverkühn in the First World War. In this novel, Germany is Faust, and is inviting damnation. 'Our "thousand-year" history, refuted, reduced *ad absurdum*, weighed in the balance and found unblest, turns out to be a road leading nowhere, or rather into despair, an unexampled bankruptcy, a *descensus Averno* lighted by the dance of roaring flames.'[11] (Both empire and the historical bankruptcy with its heaps of meaningless paper money are facts which recall the fictions of *Faust*.)

Goethe's Faust is saved because of his energy and striving. Mann's Faust is damned, though there is a shiver of equivocation – he can say, like the Faust of the *Faustbuch*, 'I die a good and a bad Christian.' Zeitblom can see a hope for his Germany, as 'clung round by demons, a hand over one eye, with the other staring into horrors, down she flings from despair to despair.'[12] The *descensus Averno* is from Aeneas' descent to the Underworld in Virgil's *Aeneid* – from where he returns living, as does Dante from the *Inferno*. Mann uses Dante's invocation to his Muse[13] as an epigraph to his novel, and this too is a glimmer of hope. The Faust story, a tale of a compromise with the forces of destruction and mockery in pursuit of knowledge, of art, of wisdom, is still a story to conjure with.

A. S. Byatt

NOTES

1   See David Constantine's Introduction for some historical details.
2   Goethe, *Poetry and Truth*, Part II, Book 10.
3   Elizabeth M. Butler, *The Fortunes of Faust* (Pennsylvania University Press, 1952; reprinted Sutton Press, 1998).
4   See The Writing of *Faust*, Schiller to Goethe, 23 June 1797.
5   Ibid.

6   T. J. Reed, *Goethe* (Oxford University Press, 1984).

7   'I have no peace', see 'Gretchen's Room', 3374.

8   Harold Bloom, *The Western Canon* (Papermac, 1995), chapter 9.

9   Dostoevsky, *The Brothers Karamazov*, chapter 9.

10   Erich Heller, *The Ironic German* (Secker and Warburg, 1958), chapter 7.

11   Thomas Mann, *Doctor Faustus*, chapter 43.

12   Ibid., final paragraph.

13   Dante, *Inferno*, Canto 2, lines 1–9.

Chronology

1749 *28 August*, Johann Wolfgang Goethe born into a well-to-do family in Frankfurt am Main.

1752–65 Goethe privately educated. He has tutors in French, Hebrew, Italian, English. His early reading: the poetry of Klopstock, Homer in translation, the Bible, French classical dramatists.

1755 Lisbon Earthquake.

1756–63 Seven Years War.

1765–8 At the University of Leipzig reading Law and a good deal else. Friendships and love affairs (Käthchen Schönkopf), many poems in rococo style, his first comedies. First readings of Shakespeare.

1768 *8 June*, Winckelmann, historian and enthusiastic apologist of Classical art, murdered in Trieste. *August 1768–March 1770*, Goethe mostly at home in Frankfurt, often ill. Interest in alchemy, association with Pietists.

1770–71 Student in Strasbourg; in love with Friederike Brion; friendship with Herder; who directed him to folksongs and ballads, reading Shakespeare, Ossian, Homer. The breakthrough into his own poetic voice. In Frankfurt and Wetzlar. The first version of *Götz von Berlichingen*, a drama in 'Shakespearian' style, written in six weeks. Some legal, more literary activity. He writes the first of poems of his *Sturm und Drang*.

1771 *14 January*, execution of Susanna Brandt for infanticide.

1772–5 (possibly even earlier) First phase of work on *Faust*.

1774 He writes and publishes his epistolary novel *Werther*. *Götz* staged in Berlin. Vast success of *Werther*.

1775 In love with Lili Schönemann, engagement to her. Journey to Switzerland. His drama *Egmont* begun. Invited to Weimar, to enter the service of Duke Karl August. Breaks off his engagement. *November*, arrives in Weimar and meets Charlotte von Stein.

1776 Herder moves to Weimar. Goethe becomes a servant of the State. Interest in the silver mines in Ilmenau; beginnings of his geological studies.

1776–86 Increasingly engaged in duties of the State (ennobled 1782); journeys on business and for pleasure to the Harz Mountains, Berlin, Switzerland; involvement with Charlotte von Stein; work for the Weimar Court Theatre; scientific studies. Many poems, work on the novel *Wilhelm Meister*, the plays *Iphigenie auf Tauris* and *Tasso*. Things unfinished, frustration and a feeling of confinement.

1786 *September*, flight to Italy. *29 October*, arrives in Rome.

1786–8 In Italy: Rome, Naples, Sicily, Rome. Lives among artists; studies to become one. The making of his classicism. *Iphigenie* recast in verse. *Egmont* finished. Further work on *Tasso* and *Faust*.

1788–90 Second phase of work on *Faust*.

1788 *18 June*, back in Weimar. Released from most of his State duties. *12 July*, begins living with Christiane Vulpius. *September*, the first of the *Roman Elegies*, which, in classical style, celebrate love and Rome; work on *Tasso*.

1789 French Revolution. *Tasso* completed. *25 December*, birth of a son, August, their only surviving child.

1790 *March–June*, second Italian journey (Venice) a disappointment. Publication of *Faust. A Fragment*.

1791 Becomes Director of the Weimar Court Theatre.

1792 Goethe at the Battle of Valmy, with Duke Karl August, on the side of the Prussians against the Revolutionary armies of France.

1793 *21 January*, execution of Louis XVI. *May–July*, again with Karl August and the Prussians, at the Siege of Mainz.

1794 Beginning of friendship and correspondence with Schiller.

1795 *Roman Elegies* published; they give offence.

1796 The verse epic *Hermann und Dorothea*, the novel *Wilhelm Meister's Apprentice Years*.

1797 Ballads, with Schiller. In Switzerland again.

1797–1801 Most of the third phase of work on *Faust*.

1798–9 Poems in classical metres (including the unfinished epic *Achilleis*).

1799 Schiller moves to Weimar.

1800–1805 Poems; a great deal of scientific work.

1805 Death of Schiller. Goethe ill, withdrawn, depressed.

1806 *14 October*, Battle of Jena, defeat of the Prussians; French troops in Weimar. *19 October*, Goethe marries Christiane Vulpius.

1807–9 Relationship with Minna Herzlieb; the novel *Elective Affinities*; work on *Wilhelm Meister's Years of Travel*, which is the continuation of the *Apprentice Years*. Begins work on the autobiography, *Poetry and Truth*. Received by Napoleon; awarded the Cross of the Legion of Honour.

1808 *Faust, Part I* published.

1812 Goethe meets Beethoven. The French retreat from Moscow.

1814–18 Relationship with Marianne von Willemer; poems of the *West-Eastern Divan*, an abundant collection.

1815 Battle of Waterloo.

1816 *6 June*, death of Christiane.

1816–17 Publication of the *Italian Journey*, from notes, diaries and letters of 1786–8.

1821 *Wilhelm Meister's Years of Travel* published.

1823–4 In love with Ulrike von Levetzow; the poems of *Trilogy of Passion*. From 1823, conversations with Johann Peter Eckermann, who will publish them after Goethe's death.

1825–31 Continues work on *Faust, Part II*.

1832 *22 March*, death of Goethe. *Faust, Part II* published posthumously.

Introduction

Goethe did not read Christopher Marlowe's *Tragical History of Doctor Faustus* until 1818, ten years after he had published his own *Faust, Part I*, and then only in a German translation; but by a curious route and in a strange guise Marlowe had visited him much earlier. Faust, the literary figure, had a shadowy historical forebear, around 1500, in one Georg Faust, a wandering charlatan with a line in horoscopes and magic, who came, it seems, to a sticky end. The fantastic tales then attaching themselves to his name were published in a chapbook, the *Historia von D. Johann Fausten*, in Frankfurt in 1587 and frequently republished, in varying editions, till the eighteenth century. The first extant English translation dates from 1592 and carries the glorious title: *The Historie of the Damnable Life, and Deserved Death of Doctor John Faustus, newly imprinted, and in convenient places imperfect matter amended: according to the true copie printed at Franckfort, and translated into English by P.F., gent.* This, or some lost and perhaps only manuscript version of it, was the source Marlowe used for his play, the first dramatization of the subject and the foundation of its importance in European literature. Exported to England in a chapbook, Faust returned to Germany in a crude version of Marlowe's drama, through the agency of English actors who toured the country during the seventeenth century. From them he passed into the repertoire of the native puppet-theatre, and it was there, in childhood, that Goethe first encountered him.

Faust accompanied Goethe throughout his life. As a literary project, which is to say as a bundle of papers, he travelled with

Goethe and always occupied some corner of his house. He was
a presence who, though for long periods dormant, could always
be summoned up or might intrude. Goethe first conceived the
play in the early 1770s, in his own early twenties, and published
Part I more than thirty years later; but he must not be thought
of as working at or being preoccupied with the project intensely
and sustainedly throughout that time. His work on *Faust* was
quite unlike Joyce's seven years on *Ulysses*, seventeen on *Finne-
gan's Wake*, or Proust's twelve on *A la recherche du temps
perdu*. Instead, and very characteristically, he took up the pro-
ject when friends or circumstances or his own needs, or a
combination of all three, drove him to it; and then let it lie
again.

Work on *Faust, Part I* went forward in three distinct phases:
1772–5, 1788–90 and 1797–1801 (and 1806). Since the
author in each phase, though still the same biographical entity,
was a very different being, changing accordingly towards his
subject, we must look at the writing and the circumstances of
each phase in turn.

Goethe was to a large extent both the chief maker and best
representative of the successive periods of mainstream German
literature in his lifetime; and writers after him suffered under
the anxiety of his influence. So his work in the early 1770s,
including that on *Faust*, not only falls within, it actually consti-
tutes the period known in German as *Sturm und Drang* (Storm
and Stress). The hallmark of that period, which had its last
and perhaps most characteristic expression in Schiller's *The
Robbers* (1782), was the rebelliousness of young men against a
society which had no room or role for their energies and talents.
They had little political impact, but revolutionized their native
literature. Goethe, always chief among them, outgrew the phase
and looked without sympathy on others still struggling in it. In
the lyric, after a rather blasé beginning in the old rococo tra-
dition, he broke through into what Keats, fifty years later (in a
letter to J. H. Reynolds, 21 September 1819), would call 'the
true voice of feeling', poems in his own right, out of his own
lived circumstances; but also, directed by the preacher and
literary critic Johann Gottfried Herder, five years his senior, he

listened to and appropriated the true popular voice, in ballads and folksongs. In drama, high on Shakespeare, he dramatized the story of Götz von Berlichingen of the Iron Hand, a sixteenth-century robber knight in whom he saw his own energy and self-assertiveness. In the novel, he created in Werther the very type of the sentimental tragic hero. In the three genres – lyric, dramatic, epic – Goethe did work that was at once very heterogeneous and of a piece; and his *Faust* is characteristic of that context.

Marlowe discerned through the fog of the legend a figure whom he could take seriously as one engaged on a dangerous and forbidden course, a man of his own bent and times; Goethe was similarly attracted. He had a pantheon of such heroes: Götz, from the same century; Prometheus; Mahomet; figures like great rivers (a favourite image), carving out courses of their own. In the case of Faust (and Götz), Goethe seems to have proceeded rather as Marlowe did, by dramatizing an existent chronicle. He read a *Faust* chapbook of 1725.

But Goethe's work on *Faust* either at once or very soon included another strand which, at that stage, he could follow through more thoroughly and consequentially than he could the story of Faust himself. This was the Gretchen tragedy. I shall say more on the joining of Faust and Gretchen later. Here it is enough to indicate that in her story Goethe had the stuff of ballads and his treatment of it was very ballad-like.

Of the two materials, Faust and Gretchen, the young Goethe composed a substantial fragmentary drama. That version, known as the *Urfaust*, was not discovered and published until 1887. It had survived in a manuscript made by Luise von Göchhausen, a lady-in-waiting at the court of Duke Karl August, in Weimar. Settling there in 1775, Goethe had read aloud from his *Faust* papers; she borrowed them and, with or without his knowledge, made a copy.

Urfaust is of great importance in the history of German literature. Published in 1887 it belongs, by its date of composition, at the start of the alternative line in German drama, the 'open' or 'neo-Shakespearean' line, which, deriving from the English Elizabethans, runs through *Sturm und Drang* (Goethe's own *Götz* and dramas by J. M. R. Lenz) to Georg Büchner, his *Danton's Death* (1835) but more particularly his *Woyzeck* (written 1836–7), also fragmentary and not published till 1879. That is the tradition Bertolt Brecht attached himself to, in opposition to the line dominantly established by the classical Goethe and Schiller. The fragmentariness of *Urfaust* and *Woyzeck*; their dramatization of a chronicle or contemporary event; their way of telling a story in intensely realized, rather disconnectedly juxtaposed single scenes (like the stanzas of a ballad); their potent use of songs: all these elements were taken up by Brecht into the theory and practice of his Epic Theatre.

In September 1786, by now aged thirty-seven and after nearly eleven years in Weimar, Goethe fled to Italy, telling nobody, not even his employer Karl August nor his friend and intimate confidante Charlotte von Stein, until, writing from Rome, he could present them with a *fait accompli*. His flight, which Karl August soon generously sanctioned, was his necessary bid for the recovery of himself as a poet. He had become, he feared, more courtier and functionary than poet; and his relationship with Charlotte, at first a productive force in his poetic life, now only stifled him. He took with him to Italy bundles of his writings, the *Faust* papers included, to prepare them (the already published and the unpublished) for a proposed *Collected Works*. But even this project seemed to him, initially at least, like the laying of a sepulchral lid on his achievements to date, rather than any new beginning. He almost shared the view of his contemporaries, that, as a writer, he was finished and had only to gather in what he had already done. All that changed in Italy. Again and again he speaks of the experience there as one of rebirth, of the rediscovery of his essential self and its vast extension into the vitally new. His taking up *Faust* again should be seen in that context, as an act of reconnection with his best, most energetic, most poetic self, and its pushing forward, into the new. He returned to *Faust* as part of the return to himself, though fifteen years on he was much changed. He was, he wrote, restored to the level of his former existence, and there felt fit to deal with *Faust* again. He was his old self, but vitally engaged in a great shift and metamorphosis too. When he took out the *Faust* papers, already yellowed and dog-eared, such a jumble, they seemed to him like the chronicle of a previous age, so that his return to them was, he said, akin to his first steeping himself in the remote historical period of Faust himself. That moment is very characteristic of Goethe: at once a reconnection, a feeling his way back into and recovery of a former stratum, the best, his youthfulness, his old energy; all that and a decisive moving forward; a truthful saying yes to what he always had been, still was and was becoming. In that strange scene the 'Witch's Kitchen', composed, incongruously enough, in the garden of the Villa Borghese in Rome, Faust is shown an arche-typal image of female beauty, into the proper appreciation of which Goethe himself, released from Frau von Stein, was just beginning to be inducted, by a young woman in Rome. Back in Weimar then, determined to go his own way, he took up with the beautiful and socially unacceptable Christiane Vulpius, had her home to live with him as his – till 1806 – unmarried wife, and wrote for her and because of her the twenty-four classical poems of the *Roman Elegies*, beautifully, gloriously giving offence to the hidebound Christian 'morality' of his day.

Still, in this second phase of work, Goethe was unable to finish *Faust*; 'the great lacuna' (between lines 605 and 1860); in which Mephistopheles and Faust were to meet and their relationship was to be determined, still could not be filled; and Goethe resigned himself to publishing the strange amalgam of his early and later endeavours as *Faust. A Fragment* in 1790, in Volume 7 of the *Collected Works*.

It was seven years before Goethe returned to *Faust*. The agent then was Schiller. At the start of their friendship, in 1794, Schiller had prompted him towards the work, calling it 'the torso of Hercules', after a famous broken statue to be seen in Rome, and urging him to complete it. But Goethe resisted, saying, 'I don't dare untie the package in which he is imprisoned.' Then in June 1797, in a restless state, he sum-moned up the necessary courage. The poem 'Dedication', writ-ten in that month, aptly conveys his sense of being almost helplessly delivered up to both a visitation and an obligation. Once begun, he worked hard at it, engaging Schiller, on the theoretical level at least, in an active collaboration. Their exchanges were part of their ongoing reflection in these years on the nature and function of the arts in society. While Goethe struggled with *Faust*, Schiller was producing his own great drama *Wallenstein*, encouraged in this by Goethe. But Schiller was through and through a tragic dramatist, which Goethe was not. Their differences, at this time of close and competitive collaboration, are very apparent in the work each produced.

Goethe's interventions during this third phase were drastic. He finished the play, its first part at least; but altered and complicated it far more than he had during his second phase of work. He both shaped and misshaped it – into something very peculiar and quite without the classical unity of purpose and execution that Schiller, in his work, was striving for and achieving at precisely the same time. Goethe filled in 'the great lacuna', added two prologues (or three if we count the poem 'Dedication'), and with the one in Heaven swung the whole concept into a new perspective. He versified all the scenes (except 'Black Day. Field') that still remained in the *Urfaust*'s prose, supplied what was missing in Gretchen's tragedy (chiefly the killing of her brother), and wrote the large 'Walpurgis Night' with its lengthy Intermezzo. Nearly all of this was done by 1801. In addition Goethe drew up a scheme for the continuation and completion of *Faust* in a second part, and wrote a sketch of the important Helena episode. When he seemed not to be proceeding single-mindedly enough, Schiller engineered a further prompting, through the publisher Cotta: the offer of another *Collected Works*. And Goethe did indeed exert himself towards that opportunity. He was ready, after last revisions, by April 1806; but then in October, at the Battle of Jena, the Revolutionary wars came very close, delaying everything. One sad irony is that Schiller, without whom, almost certainly, Goethe would never have finished *Faust*, still only saw it as a work in progress. He died in 1805, three years before the publication of *Faust, Part I* in Volume 8 of the new *Collected Works*.

So much for the genesis of the first part of Goethe's *Faust* (but
see also the notes on individual scenes). We now have to ask
whether such a long, complex and highly idiosyncratic compo-
sition shows in the finished drama and should affect our reading
and understanding of it. There are two schools of thought. One:
that Goethe unified and homogenized the whole thing as he
worked; accordingly, we need pay little or no attention to its
genesis as we read. Two: that he didn't (couldn't or wouldn't),
and that the play is everywhere marked (if not flawed) by the
manner of its composition, which we are bound in our reading
to take into account. Though I am of that latter school, and
it informs this Introduction, the Notes and perhaps even the
translation, I am not so extreme in it that I deny the whole any
unity at all. But having some critical sense of how Goethe
actually worked at *Faust* is, in my view, more helpful to our
reading than having none. The Unitarian School has to strain
very piously indeed to make everything, even just in *Part I*,
fit; and I think that constant strain very detrimental to our
reading.

Finishing *Part II*, and thus the whole work, Goethe himself
more than once referred to his *Faust* as something 'incommen-
surable'; by which I think he meant that the component parts of
it had no common standard of measurement among themselves;
also perhaps that the work was so peculiar that it would be
hard to find criteria by which it could be usefully compared
with anything else. Indeed, he even asserted (to his confidant
and chronicler Johann Peter Eckermann, 6 May 1827) that the
more incommensurable and elusive to the understanding a
work of literature is, the better it is. He had said much the same
about his novel *Elective Affinities*, which, like *Faust*, baffled
and divided his contemporaries: 'das Gedichtete behauptet sein
Recht', which is to say, the literary work has its own way of
being right, its own rights, which it asserts. Then, although he
was clear as he worked on *Part II* that it could not be allowed
to be as 'fragmentary' (his own word) as *Part I*, still his verdict
on the completed whole was that it was inevitably fragmentary.
Much earlier, when acceding to Schiller's wish that he take up
the project again, he spoke of allowing it to come into being

like a large family of fungi. Or, using less organic imagery, he spoke repeatedly of 'fitting it together'. All in all, by his own assessment, each part of *Faust* and certainly the two together, should be read as a containment of incommensurables, not at all harmonious and unified but intriguing and productive in its very contradictions. And also as fragmentary; that is, the fragments of it, 'put together' into a whole incommensurable work, have a good deal of autonomy, they make vital sense in themselves. Goethe thought his *Faust* a strange, hybrid and wondrous work, and foretold, quite correctly, that earnest readers seeking a coherent sense in it would be mystified. It lives in its 'contraries', and in them it is very lively indeed.

Some incommensurables in *Faust* are due to its spasmodic composition over thirty years. Others were there at the outset, in the whole fraught nexus of the play, in the very meeting of Goethe with the Faust material. Or we should say that the long composition actually *brought out* the incommensurables, the contradictions, inherent in the enterprise from the start. It was with good reason that Goethe left gaps during the first two phases of work. He could not see how to fill them. Then as he did fill them, some irreconcilable elements were brought to light; others were actually brought into being. Goethe took up the Faust story as something that was at once attractive and repellent. Like Marlowe (only more so), he could sympathize with the hero's restlessness, impatience and desire to transgress; but, like Gotthold Ephraim Lessing (1729–81), his immediate German predecessor in the treatment of Faust's story, he would have no truck with the idea of damnation. In fact, Goethe several times took up subjects whose original or inherent tendency he was bound, by his very nature, to oppose. The story of Iphigenia in Tauris, for example, or the brief life of Achilles after the death of Hector. In both he opposed the Greek idea of fate: it left too little room for human autonomy. On the subject of Achilles he tried an epic poem, as a sort of sequel to Homer's *Iliad*, and failed almost completely; and he dealt with Iphigenia in a five-act drama which Schiller thought 'astonishingly modern and un-Greek'. Goethe's *Faust* is astonishingly modern and, contradicting its origins, unchristian. Every writer taking up a traditional myth will fight for his or her own identity against it. Goethe, the most receptive and impressionable of writers, was at the same time quite exceptionally self-assured; and in that twin capacity he opened himself up to and *contradicted* the story of Faust.

But the contradiction was not a single antithesis to a given thesis. The material itself, highly attractive in some respects, repellent in others, made for a multiplicity of response, which the long genesis, the changing idea, then further complicated.

We can study this dynamism in two large instances, which are really two in one: the Gretchen tragedy, and Faust's wager or pact with Mephistopheles. The latter (as a pact) is the very basis of the old legend. The former, though perhaps originally a separate interest, was very soon, and without there being any equivalent in the traditional material, brought by Goethe into Faust's orbit. It was an uneasy meeting. Gretchen's story – the girl seduced and abandoned, killing her baby – is itself traditional. It is the stuff of ballads, and, with or without the infanticide, of a good deal of eighteenth-century European theatre. There was also, in 1772 in Goethe's home town of Frankfurt, a particular example of the social realities behind that tradition. A young unmarried woman by the name of Susanna Margaretha Brandt killed her baby and the Law beheaded her for it. Goethe's interest was no doubt further quickened by his own bad conscience over his dealings with women, notably Friederike Brion, whom he had broken with in 1771. That mix – a literary tradition and a strong social and personal actuality – is very typical of Goethe, and is enough, in the case of Gretchen's story, to make a powerful and autonomous drama. But when it is yoked to Faust's traditional dealings with the Devil, whether understood as wager or pact, the Gretchen story is thrown into a quite different light. Gretchen and her fate are thereby subordinated to Faust's, she is reduced to a thing having instrumental value, she becomes an item in his whole career, an agent, always essentially subservient to him and the 'main plot' of his salvation or damnation. The 'Prologue in Heaven' (242 ff.), condemned by some early British critics for its 'blasphemous levity', has, like the Book of Job it derives from, a very cold heart to it. Faust himself is the subject of a bet; Gretchen is then instrumentalized into a part of it. Viewed from that vantage point, Faust and Gretchen are like the characters in *Elective Affinities*, the subjects of an experiment, the ironic tone of the novel being much the same as that of the 'Prologue', only a few degrees colder.

In the old Faust books, and in Marlowe's play, Faust enters into a pact. The Devil serves him for twenty-four years and, when that period is over, carries him off to hell. Nothing so definite occurs in Goethe's version. Altogether, in his treatment of this central and defining moment of the old story, he inclines to trivialization, irony and a very characteristic blurring or fudging of the issue (the ending of *Faust II* – not surprisingly, given this premise – is a masterpiece of just that). When Mephisto (in 'Faust's Study (II)', 1529 ff.) offers a pact such as Faust (in the previous scene) has indicated he might wish to make, Faust pays scant regard to what the consequences would be for him if he accepts; doubts very much if Mephisto could deliver what he desires; and (1692 ff.) instead of a pact proposes a wager – not at all the same thing as a pact whose outcome, whatever his conduct, is agreed and certain. In the wager, he will only pay the forfeit if he loses. He feels sure he won't lose, but also seems not to care tuppence about the forfeit – falling to Mephistopheles – if he does. His contempt (and Goethe's) for the old rigmarole and ceremony of the deal, especially the signing in blood, indicates the difficulty and embarrassment inherent in this meeting of a sixteenth-century legend and an eighteenth-century humane intelligence.

Nonetheless, the wager Faust offers Mephisto, however little he cares about the consequences if he loses, *is* significant and, applied to the Gretchen story, it is pretty chilling. Faust loses if he ever bids a moment stay; that is, if he ever feels happy and satisfied in the present. He wins if he remains perpetually disappointed. You might say, if the threat of damnation is to be taken at all seriously, that he avoids it in the afterlife by being damned already in the way he lives on earth. A man living as Faust does is – in an existentialist sense – already in hell.

Faust is driven along in the constant expectation of disappointment; and if he is to win his wager, he must actually will it. To win, he must treat all human relations, all human experience, as stuff for disappointment. If he longs for and strives for satisfaction in the here and now, with anybody, doing anything, he is willing and striving for his own damnation. Living by the steady will to disappointment, the way of death in life if ever there was one, he will win his wager and avoid the traditional damnation.

Faust replicates on his human level the wager of which he, from the Lord's and Mephisto's point of view, is himself a part. In Gretchen we see the consequences close up. To win, if we take the wager seriously, Faust must demonstrate that human life, epitomized in her, disappoints him. She will be the material proof. I say 'if we take the wager seriously' because, once the Gretchen story is under way, the force of it, its own integrity, carries Faust (and us) along. Surely there must be moments in it to which, in truth, he would have to say, 'Bide here, you are so beautiful'. Since he never does and Mephisto never challenges him, we have to assume that the affair is unfailingly and manifestly disappointing; or that Goethe, author and overseer but himself being carried along, forgets it.

In any view of the whole work, certainly if we take the two parts together, no such welcome and convenient forgetting is possible. The two wagers, the first in Heaven, the second in Faust's study, haunt the whole play; and their spirit is, in my view, desolating. Faust's fellow human beings, principally and unforgettably Gretchen, are so much material in his personal enterprise. They are the stuff by which he proves something. It would not make it any better if his premises and driving force were moral ones, of course; but it is at least worth pointing out that they are not. 'Striving', famously (very quotably) adduced by a chorus of angels at the conclusion of *Part II*, as a 'saving grace', is in fact a wholly amoral category. As an absolute energy – merely striving, without stated aim or direction – it is no more moral or immoral, but in Faust's practice a good deal more harmful, than running on the spot. Merely being unsatisfied, merely insisting and proving that life is a continual disappointment, cannot possibly, in any scheme of morals or religion, be in any sense redemptive. It is manifestly – for all the Christian ethos of the original and for all the Christian paraphernalia of the final curtain – not Christian. But nor is it 'Goethean'. Goethe, though a restless and ever-changing man, certainly did not seek to prove life disappointing. On the contrary, he sought his happiness in it, and by all accounts, autobiographical and poetic, frequently found his happiness in it. So he is not one and the same with his hero. Faust, insufferable enough in his loquacious egotism, becomes – by the wager he enters into with Mephisto, by the view of human life which that wager entails and by the way he lives – perhaps the least sympathetic 'hero' in world literature. Small wonder that his author, principally through Mephisto, often sides against him.

Faust has as its subtitle: 'A Tragedy'. *Is* it? The question is not entirely academic and, whether it can be answered or not, the very uncertainty is significant, and a further pointer towards Goethe's complicated and resistant attitude towards his material. The *Urfaust* Gretchen story is tragic, as consequentially so as *Werther*. It moves inexorably, scene by scene, episode by episode, to its bitter end. At that stage of composition it is Gretchen's tragedy; but once incorporated into *Part I*, she and her fate are subordinated to the central issue, Faust's wager; and because she is not only judged (as in *Urfaust*) but also, according to a voice from above ('Prison', 4611), saved, she is, so to speak, on the grand scale at least, put safely to one side for use at the conclusion of *Part II*, when, as 'Una Poenitentium', she intercedes for Faust. But did Goethe actually believe in the Higher Instance who in *Part I* of his play declares her saved? That question involves the larger one: how seriously does Goethe take, there and at the end of *Part II*, the whole Christian superstructure of salvation or damnation?

Since, in the end, neither Gretchen nor her guilty lover are damned, the whole play cannot be thought tragic in the way that Marlowe's is. There a man follows his hubris and pays an ultimate price. He sees Christ's blood streaming in the firmament and is denied its saving grace. There was never the least chance that Goethe would finish his play at all like that. In the 'Prologue in Heaven' the Lord actually incorporates Mephistopheles into a divine economy whose outcome will be good (337 ff.); Mephisto himself, oddly enough, does much the same (in 'Faust's Study (I)', 1336–7). We may add this pre-established harmony to the other incommensurables in the play, but they are in themselves very characteristic of Goethe after his *Sturm und Drang*. He said of himself more than once that his nature was conciliatory. After *Werther* and *Urfaust* he looked for ways of avoiding the terrible cul-de-sac into which a truly tragic action leads. Thus in his handling of the Iphigenia story he sought the humane get-out: his heroine trusts her 'barbarian' counterpart, King Thoas, to act like a gentleman, and he does. And for his drama *Tasso*, his novel *Elective Affinities* and *Faust* Goethe devised endings that resist all unambiguous categorization.

I should say that Goethe, 'the old heathen', caring as little about the afterlife as his Faust did, concentrates his interest on the life being lived on earth. *Faust* then is the tragedy of a man living badly, according to a perverse and harmful idea. Goethe demonstrates the harm that he does to himself and to others. The ending of *Part II*, which is, like that of the *Elective Affinities*, more radiant with irony than with grace, matters much less than does the study of the lives lived prior to it.

Translator's Note

It was Madame de Stael, in her *De l'Allemagne* (published and at once translated in London in 1813), who directed the British reading public to the achievements of recent German literature, among them Goethe's *Faust*; and translations of parts and of the whole of it soon began to appear in periodicals and in book form. Shelley, probably in 1815 or 1816, translated the first thousand or so lines, in a very literal and inaccurate fashion, chiefly, it seems, as a way of teaching himself the language and certainly not for publication. Then in 1822, the year he drowned, he did poetically compelling, though not always accurate, versions of 'Prologue in Heaven' and 'Walpurgis Night'. A bibliography of whole or partial translations and adaptations, compiled by William Heinemann in 1882, has at least one entry, and often half a dozen, for almost every year from 1820. The American scholar Adolf Ingram Frantz, writing in 1949, considered nearly fifty substantial translations of *Faust I* and/ or *Faust II*; and since then there have been many more.

In their own language, sprung from and indelibly marked by their own time and place, literary works live on, generation after generation. Their inherent vitality, and their being vital to us, ensures their survival. But most translations are nowhere near so long-lived: they last a while, serve a purpose, and die. The purpose they serve is a necessary one, and not ignoble. They convey the original work, they bear it along, they help disseminate it; they do this for a time then fall away, and other translations are needed to sustain and continue the life of the work itself.

My predecessor in Penguin, Philip Wayne, published his

translation of *Part I* in 1949 and of *Part II* ten years later. They have been in print ever since. He was besides an editor of Shakespeare and Wordsworth; he made anthologies of English letters, of verses for children and of one-act plays, and wrote a couple of nature books as well. He was headmaster of St Marylebone Grammar School, and in that capacity is affectionately remembered by a former pupil, Eric Hobsbawm, émigré from Hitler's Germany, in his autobiography *Interesting Times*. So far as I know, Philip Wayne's only other translation is of a comedy by the historical Faust's near-contemporary, Hans Sachs. His *Faust*, so soon after the War, is one of many courageous efforts by British writers, publishers and the BBC to reconnect with the humane European tradition in Germany's culture that Hitler had sought to annihilate.

Every translator of *Faust* must feel the predecessors crowding round. In making my attempt, I followed my usual practice. I didn't read or consult anybody else's version until I was sure of my own; that is, until I was sure of my own slant and voice and would be immune against anybody else's. Then I assembled three or four predecessors and line by line read them against what I had written. So I had their critical scrutiny, they showed me where my understanding of Goethe was doubtful or had gone astray and where I must, in my own way, correct it. After that, I got my version read by three or four people whose opinions on language, particularly on the language of poetry, I trust. Their readings were quite indispensable. A translator struggles to carry over the whole liveliness of the foreign text; failure is certain. But to all those who helped me 'fail better', I am very grateful.

The long tradition of failure was initiated by Lord Francis Leveson Gower, in 1825. He translated Goethe's text into English verse, omitting, often without notice, such passages as he either could not do or thought indecent. In the passages he thought he *could* do, he made innumerable basic errors. This was pointed out, quite mercilessly, by a linguistically far more competent successor, Abraham Hayward, in 1835. Hayward translated into English prose, and justified that decision on grounds that are at once interesting and wholly unpersuasive.

Faust, he wrote, 'teems with thought, and has long exercised a widely-spread influence by qualities wholly independent of metre and rhyme'. Accordingly, Hayward employed prose for his translation and is accurate in rendering the lexical sense of Goethe's lines. Indeed, in accompanying notes he discusses his own and other people's translations, usefully indicating real lexical difficulties. But he is quite wrong in his premise. Nothing in *Faust* works independently of metre and rhyme, nor is *Faust* a great work because of its 'thought'. Its 'thought', whatever that might be, exists and is effective by virtue of a literary language which, after the rewriting of *Urfaust*, is, but for one short scene, verse. Goethe himself warned us off trying to get at *Faust* as though it were an assemblage of rational thoughts. The liveliness of the text, its peculiar vitality and why it is vital to us is a product of its poetry. A prose version may do some service, help us understand the lexical sense; but in the chief endeavour, the conveying of the peculiar liveliness of the original, it fails automatically by being prose.

So, like most recent predecessors, I have attempted to put Goethe's text into English verse. I am not a 'mimetic' translator; that is, I don't seek always to reproduce the *means* by which in German Goethe achieves his effects. Instead, I try for equivalence of effect, by whatever means I have at my disposal in the English language. In practice, because the rough or smooth iambic lines which are the chief medium of Goethe's play are available and do work similarly in English, I have often mirrored them; but mimesis was never my first principle. In rhyming (which, as a principal poetic resource in Goethe's language, could not possibly be dispensed with in English) I have allowed myself two liberties. First, I have used a great deal of half-rhyme and compensatory assonance. This is a well-established practice in contemporary British verse and I saw no reason to try to manage without it. And secondly, though I rhyme as often as Goethe does, I do not always place my rhymes where his are. This allowed me to shift around for a less constrained or more forceful expression. But if I judged the placing of his rhymes to be particularly important, that is actually engendering vital effects, then I was careful to follow him closely. Thus whenever characters rhyme across the dialogue, or when rhymes bring about a striking irony or resolution, I either placed mine exactly where his are or, if I allowed myself any leeway, sought hard to produce an effect analogous to the one I had detected in his German.

That latter strategy, doing here what you cannot do there, is known in the trade as 'compensation'. A translator performs countless little acts of compensation all the time, and really it will be best to think of the whole undertaking, from the first line to the last, as one sustained act of compensation. In a translation you are constantly seeking to devise means by which you may at least approach the innate liveliness of the original. This is, I think, what Coleridge meant in the Preface to his translation of Schiller's *Wallenstein*: 'Translation of poetry into poetry is difficult, because the Translator must give a brilliancy to his language without that warmth of original conception, from which such brilliancy would follow of its own accord.' A translator is almost bound to trail behind and not just because of the unbridgeable gap of talent, but also because translation by its very nature must seek to engender effects, always closely following the original, which, as Coleridge says, came more naturally out of the native fire of that original. The aim is always to write an English verse which, whilst conveying the whole freight of sense and implication of the original, will be readable with pleasure as English verse – and as verse, more-over, that the reader reading now will feel to be the language of his or her day and age, the language in which the real concerns of the present age are being addressed in verse which is not translation. Pastiche, antiquarian harking back, belated language will not do. The original itself will be felt to belong in the museum if that is where the translator's language comes from. Trendiness will not work either, since much up-to-the-minute language will be dead in an hour.

It has been statistically proved that the language of transla-tion is, most often, less *various* than the language of original composition. In their syntax, vocabulary, stylistic range and registers, translators, on the whole, achieve less variety than the authors they are translating have achieved. They tend to

flatten and reduce the original. Perhaps in the wish to be readily
intelligible, to offend against none of the varieties of the ver-
nacular they are translating into, translators are drawn to a
sort of middle ground, towards a consensus. The cost of that
conscious or unconscious accommodation is very high. It saps
the original work's vitality. But knowing that risk or tendency
is one thing, countering it is quite another.

The gap between the ambition of the translator (to write
something of a kindred liveliness) and the execution will, if
anything, be even greater than the gap most poets feel between
the conception and the execution of most poems. But there is
something very potent about that very gap. In the failure itself
there is a sort of driving force. Goethe, aware of his own
tendency not to finish things, once observed encouragingly that
'falling short is itself productive'. Productive of, at least, the
desire to make up the gap. This impulse is akin to the 'want or
power' which Shelley, in his essay 'On Love', thought the very
hallmark of being human, our idealistic drive, without which
we are only a 'living sepulchre'. To make a virtue of failure
may seem like special pleading; but in the case of *Faust* at least,
where translators need all the special pleading they can get,
there is a certain attractiveness and perhaps even rightness in
the idea, since the play itself lives and moves and has its being
in a restless, fragmented, constantly metamorphosing 'want or
power'.

The text of Goethe's *Faust* is agreed and not problematic. I
have used the Hamburg edition, edited by Erich Trunz, for this
translation. I have numbered my lines to match the German.
The lines themselves, their actual content, will not always corre-
spond exactly, but they will always be close enough to the
German for a quotation to be found or a comparison of German
and English to be made.

I have been greatly helped in my thinking about *Faust*, and
so in writing my Introduction and the Notes, by Ulrich Gaier's
volume of *Erläuterungen und Dokumente* (Reclam Nr. 16021,
Stuttgart 2001), and by the editorial material accompanying
two English translations. The first of these is David Luke's

Faust. Part I in the Oxford World's Classics Series (1987; reissued 1998). He is a particularly knowledgeable and clear exponent of the genesis of Goethe's play, and altogether an astute, amusing and enlightening guide. And the second is the Norton Critical Edition of *Faust. Parts I and II* (New York, 1976; reissued 2001). The translation is by Walter Arndt, the editorial work by Cyrus Hamlin. I must also mention John Williams's translation and edition in Wordsworth Classics (1999). He is a lively translator. His volume contains not only *Part I* but also *Urfaust* and the ribald sketches that Goethe wrote for 'Walpurgis Night' but did not publish.

The Writing of *Faust*

(For a fuller account see the Introduction, pp. xxv–xxix.)

1. 1774–5

Goethe was only intermittently occupied with *Faust*. He moved to Weimar in November 1775, already by then notorious as the author of *Werther*.

Heinrich Christian Boie's diary, 15 October 1774:

> Spent the whole day alone and undisturbed with Goethe ... I made him read aloud to me, many things, some finished, some fragments, and in all of them an original voice and peculiar power and in all, however strange they may be and incorrect, there is the stamp of genius. His *Doctor Faustus* is almost finished and seems to me the greatest and most characteristic thing he has done.

Boie (1744–1806) was a jurist and minor writer, editor of several literary journals. He had some dealings with Goethe at this time.

Karl Ludwig von Knebel to Friedrich Justin Bertuch, 23 December 1774:

So much from Goethe! ... I've had a stack of fragments from him, among other things for a *Doctor Faustus*, in which there are some quite exceptionally splendid scenes. He hauls forth manuscripts from every corner of his room.

Knebel (1744–1834), translator of Lucretius and Propertius, became one of Goethe's closest friends. Bertuch (1747–1822) was a Weimar bookseller, businessman and councillor at the Court.

Goethe was visited by Friedrich Gottlieb Klopstock (1724–1803), the highly respected author of the *Messias*, in Frankfurt at the end of March 1775. This is from the account he gave of their conversations in *Poetry and Truth*, Book XVIII:

He showed me such friendliness I became open and confiding. I showed him the newest scenes from *Faust*. He seemed to like them and, moreover, as I learned later, praised them to other people with more emphasis than was usual with him, saying that he desired the completion of the work.

Goethe to Auguste, Countess of Stolberg, 17 September 1775:

The day passed in a middling sort of dullness. When I got up, I felt good and did a scene of my *Faust*. Then frittered a couple of hours away. Then flirted away another couple with a girl your brothers may tell you about, a strange creature. Ate in the company of a dozen decent enough fellows, honest as the day God made them. Rowed to and fro on the water. Teaching myself to row is my little passion at the moment ... And in all this I felt like a rat that has swallowed poison, he runs down one hole after another, guzzles anything liquid, gobbles up every eatable thing that comes his way, and all the while his insides are burning with an unquenchable and fatal fire.

Auguste (1753–1835), sister of Counts Friedrich Leopold and Christian and Countess Henriette, was a favourite correspondent of the young Goethe.

Goethe to Johann Heinrich Merck, October 1775:

> I have translated the Song of Songs, which is the most wonderful
> collection of love songs God ever made ... I am tolerably well.
> Have written a lot at *Faust*.

Merck (1741–91), writer and acerbic critic, was one of Goethe's
closest and most important friends in these years. Some say
Goethe thought of him as Mephistopheles.

Friedrich Leopold, Count of Stolberg, to his sister Henriette,
Weimar, 6 December 1775:

> One afternoon Goethe read us his half-finished *Faust*. It is a
> splendid work. The Duchesses were profoundly moved by some
> of the scenes.

Friedrich Leopold (1750–1819), poet. He and his brother
Christian toured Switzerland with Goethe in the summer
of 1775. The Duchesses are Anna-Amalia and Luise, of
Weimar.

2. *1786–90*

Goethe to Duke Karl August, Rome, middle of December
1786:

> Now I shall move on to the other things, and finally also *Faust*.
> When I decided to publish my fragments I considered myself
> dead. How happy I shall be if by finishing what I have begun I
> can prove I have come back to life.

To the same, Rome, 8 December 1787:

> I shall come to *Faust* last of all, when I've got everything else
> behind me. To finish the work, I shall have to take an extremely

firm hold on myself. I must draw a magic circle around me and
I look to good fortune to show me where best to do it.

From the chronology of Goethe's works drawn up by Ecker-
mann and Riemer, published 1837:

> 1788: Plan for going on with *Faust*. Some scenes of it written.
> The scene 'Witch's Kitchen' done in the Borghese Gardens.

Goethe, *Italian Journey*, Rome, 1 March 1788:

> I have been brave enough to give thought to my final three
> volumes all together, and I now know exactly what I wish to do.
> May heaven send me the mood and the luck to do it! It was a
> rich week, more like a month when I look back on it. – First I
> did the plan for *Faust,* and that operation was, I hope, a success.
> Of course, it is quite another matter completing the work now
> rather than fifteen years ago. But I think nothing will be lost,
> especially since I believe that now I have found the thread again.
> Also I am reassured as to the tone of the whole. I have already
> written one new scene, and if I were to smoke the pages I think
> nobody would be able to pick them out from among the old.
> Through the long period of quiet and isolation here I have been
> brought back fully to the level of my own existence, and it is
> remarkable how much I am still the same and how little my inner
> being has suffered from the years and all that has happened. The
> sight of the old manuscript troubles me sometimes. It is still the
> same one. The chief scenes are just as they were when I first
> hurried them to paper without any plan or draft. By now it is so
> yellowed with age, so ill-used (the sheets were never bound), so
> dog-eared and delicate that truly it resembles a fragment of some
> ancient codex. And just as then I had to think and imagine myself
> back into an earlier world, so now I have to put myself back
> again into a previous era of my own life.

Goethe to Duke Karl August, Weimar, 5 July 1789:

I shall publish *Faust* as a fragment, for more than one reason. I'll explain when I see you . . .

Goethe's diary, January 1790:

Sent off *Faust*.

3. *1794–1806*

The chief mover in this decisive third phase of the writing of *Faust* was Schiller, who died (in 1805) without seeing its publication.

Schiller to Goethe, 29 November 1794. Goethe has promised to send the beginning of *Wilhelm Meister's Apprentice Years*. Schiller thanks him, and adds:

But I am just as eager to read those fragments of your *Faust* that have not been published. For I confess that what I have read of the play is, to me, like the Torso of Hercules. The scenes have a power and a fullness of genius that are the unmistakable marks of the highest mastery, and I should like to follow as far as possible the large and audacious character that breathes therein.

Goethe to Schiller, 2 December 1794:

I cannot send you any *Faust* at present. I don't dare untie the parcel that imprisons him. If I copied things out, I should be bound to try to develop them, and I don't feel up to that. But if in the future anything were to make me able, it would surely be your interest and encouragement.

Goethe's diary, 5 June 1797:

After dinner, 'Oberon's Golden Wedding' [the Intermezzo in the scene 'Walpurgis Night'].

Goethe to Schiller, 22 June 1797:

Since in my present restlessness it is very necessary that I give
myself something to do, I have decided to take up my *Faust* and,
if not to finish it, at least to bring it a good bit further forward.
So I shall undo what has already been printed, sort it in large
blocks together with what else has already been written or con-
ceived, and in that way make a closer preparation for the
execution of the whole plan which, it must be said, is still only
an idea. I have now addressed this plan again, and how it might
be realized, and have pretty well reached agreement with myself.
But I wish that you, in some sleepless night, would be kind
enough to think the thing through, to lay before me the demands
that you would yourself make of the whole, and in that fashion,
like a true prophet, relate and interpret my own dreams to me. –
Since the different parts of this poem, so far as mood is concerned,
can be treated differently, just so long as they subordinate them-
selves to the spirit and the tone of the whole, and since moreover
the whole work is a subjective one, I can work at it whenever I
have a moment, and am in fact able to do something now.

Schiller to Goethe, 23 June 1797:

Your decision to work at *Faust* comes as a great surprise to me,
especially now, as you make ready for your journey to Italy. But
I have once and for all given up trying to measure you by any
usual logic and am accordingly persuaded in advance that your
genius will be quite undaunted by the business. – Your request
to me that I should tell you what my desires and expectations
might be, is not easily met. But, as well as I can, I will try to
discover your thread, and if even that proves impossible I shall
pretend I came across the fragments of *Faust* by accident and
had to finish them myself. All I will say at present is this: that
Faust (the play, I mean), for all its poetic individuality, still cannot
entirely resist the demand for symbolic significance, which is no
doubt your own idea of it also. We can never lose sight of
the contradictory double nature of humankind and the failed
endeavour to unite the divine and the physical in the human

being; and since the plot runs, and must run, into the crass and the shapeless, one will not wish to remain stuck in the subject, but will be led by it into ideas. In brief, the demands on *Faust* are at once philosophical and poetic, and you may shift as you like, the nature of the subject will nonetheless oblige you to treat it philosophically, and the imagination will have to accommodate itself in the service of an idea of the reason. – But in saying this, I am surely telling you nothing new, since in what is there already you have begun to satisfy those demands in high measure.

Goethe's diary, June 1797:

23 June. A more thorough plan for *Faust*. – 24 June. The poem 'Dedication', for *Faust* ... In the afternoon further work on *Faust*. – 26 June. Work on *Faust*. – 27 June. Work on *Faust*.

Goethe to Schiller, 24 June 1797:

I thank you for your first words on my reviving *Faust*. We shall probably not differ in our view of this work, but it is at once quite peculiarly encouraging to see my own thoughts and premises set down from outside too, and your interest is in more than one sense productive ... To begin with I shall only try to complete the large blocks that are already conceived and half worked out and to fit them together with what is published, and carry on in that fashion until the circle exhausts itself ...

Schiller to Goethe, 26 June 1797:

I have now read *Faust* again, and I feel dizzy at the welter of it. But that is very natural, since one needs a viewpoint, an idea, and in the absence of that, even a less abundant material must necessarily bewilder the rational mind. What bothers me is that *Faust*, which in its innate tendency requires totality, seems to require totality in its material also, if in the end the idea is to be shown fully worked out, and I can find no poetic glue that would hold together such a copiously seething mass. But no doubt you will find a way. – For example: It was right, in my view, that

Faust should be introduced into the life of action, and whatever piece of such material you choose, it always seems, I think, to demand too much breadth and circumstance . . . I am very eager to see how the folk tale will fit with the philosophical part of the whole.

Goethe to Schiller, 27 June 1797:

Your comments on *Faust* rejoiced me. They coincide very well, as it was natural that they should, with my own premises and plans, except that in this barbarian composition I shall not be too scrupulous: I think to touch on, rather then meet, the highest demands . . . I shall make sure the different parts are agreeable and entertaining whilst also giving food for thought . . .

Goethe to Schiller, 1 July 1797:

As far as the scheme and overview of my *Faust* are concerned, I have made large and rapid advances . . . All I want now is a quiet month and the work would push from the earth like a great family of polyps, to be a manifold wonder and horror to the world . . . I'm having what has already been published copied out again, and with gaps left between the parts, so that the new will be better able to grow together with the old.

Goethe to Schiller, 5 July 1797:

Faust is set back at present, the nordic phantoms have been pushed back by southern reminiscences for a while. But I have completed a very thorough scheme and overview of the whole.

Goethe's diary, 1798:

9 April. Began work on *Faust* again . . . – 10 April, *Faust* early. – 11 April. *Faust*. – 14 April. Towards evening did various things with *Faust* . . . – 15 April. Busied myself with *Faust*. – 18 April. Worked on *Faust*. – 19 April. Worked on *Faust*. – 21 April. Worked on *Faust*.

Goethe to Schiller, 11 April 1798:

So that the next four weeks, which I shall be spending here [Weimar], will not go by unused, I have at once taken up *Faust* again, and find your observation correct: that the mood of spring-time is lyrical, which for my rhapsodic drama is a great advantage.

Goethe to Schiller, 28 April 1798:

Thank you for Cotta's statement . . . It would be an opportunity to find a place for various things one doesn't otherwise know what to do with, and what's good for the bookseller is also in every sense good for the author. Being well paid, one is also widely read, and both prospects are pleasing . . . I shall finish my *Faust* too, which, given its nordic nature, must surely find a vast nordic readership.

Johann Friedrich Cotta (1764–1832), perhaps the most important publisher in Germany then. Goethe's chief publisher from 1806 onwards.

Goethe to Schiller, 5 May 1798:

I have made good progress with my *Faust*. The old – still extant – and extremely confused manuscript has been copied out and the different parts placed in separate folders one behind the other and numbered according to a full and detailed scheme. Now I can use any moment of my being in the mood to continue the work on particular parts and sooner or later fit the whole thing together. – One very strange thing has come to light in this: some scenes of a tragic nature were written in prose and are now, by their naturalness and power, quite unbearable in relation to the rest. For that reason I am at present trying to cast them into rhyme, for then the idea shines as it were through a veil whilst the effect of the terrible material, previously unmediated, is quietened.

Schiller to Goethe, 8 May 1798:

> I congratulate you on your progress with *Faust*. As soon as you
> know for certain what further needs doing with the material, it
> is as good as done. Its *boundlessness* always seemed to me the
> most difficult thing about it.

Schiller to Cotta, 16 December 1798:

> Goethe has a lot of work on his *Faust* still before he is finished.
> I pester him to complete it and his intention at least is to do so
> next summer . . .

Schiller to Cotta, 24 March 1800:

> Finally, a piece of advice. I am afraid that Goethe will abandon
> his *Faust*, so much of which has already been done, unless from
> outside, and by tempting propositions, he can be brought to take
> up this great work again and finish it . . . I am convinced that a
> brilliant offer coming from you might induce him to do the
> remaining work this summer . . .

Goethe to Schiller, 11 April 1800:

> Cotta's liberality is very welcome. I have had a letter from him
> on the subject of *Faust*, which is probably your doing, and which
> I am grateful for, since on this prompting I have indeed taken
> out the work again and thought it through.

Goethe's diary, 1800:

> 11 April. Letter from Cotta concerning *Faust*. – 13 April. *Faust*.
> – 14 April. *Faust*. [Such notes again and again until 5 September.]

Goethe to Schiller, 16 April 1800:

> The devil I am conjuring up is behaving very strangely.

Goethe to Schiller, 12 September 1800:

> After various adventures I have at last, early this morning, recovered the peace and quiet of Jena and I tried something at once, but with no success. Happily during this last week I was able to hold on to the scenes you know about, and my Helena has indeed made her appearance. But now I am so attracted by the beauty of the heroine's situation that I shall be sad if I must at once transform it into a joke . . .

Goethe had for many years made use of nearby Jena as a place of diversion and retreat.

Goethe's diary, 1800:

> 12 September. Early this morning Helena . . . Wrote to Counsellor Schiller about Helena. – 13 September. Helena. – 14 September. Helena. [Such notes again and again until the end of September.]

Schiller to Goethe, 13 September 1800:

> I wish you luck with the step you have taken in your *Faust*. But don't be disturbed by the thought that, when beautiful figures and situations come, it is a shame to barbarize them. There may be several more such occasions in the second part of *Faust*, and it might be a good thing to silence your poetic conscience on that score once and for all. A barbarian handling of the story, which is required of you by the spirit of the whole, cannot destroy the lofty content nor cancel out its beauty, but will rather make it specific in a different guise and appreciable by a different capacity of the soul. Precisely that which is loftier and more distinguished in the story's motifs will give the work a peculiar charm, and Helena in this play is a symbol for all the beautiful figures who will wander into it.

Goethe to Schiller, 16 September 1800:

> The consolation you offered me in your letter, that through the union of the pure and the bizarre a not wholly reprehensible poetic monster might be born, has been realized now in my own experience. For out of this amalgamation strange phenomena have come forth in which I myself take some pleasure.

Schiller to Goethe, 23 September 1800 (Schiller had visited Goethe in Jena two days before and Goethe had read him the finished part of 'Helena'):

> Your recent reading left me with the impression of something great and distinguished. The lofty and noble spirit of antique tragedy wafts out of the monologue towards the listener and has the proper effect. Calmly and powerfully it stirs up the very deepest feelings. If you brought nothing else poetic back from Jena but this and what you have decided for the further progress of this tragic part, your stay there would be rewarded. If you manage this synthesis of the noble and the barbarian, and I don't doubt that you will, the key to the rest of the whole work will also have been found, and it will not be hard for you, from this point onwards, to determine, as it were, analytically, the sense and the spirit of the remaining parts. For this peak, as you call it yourself, will surely be visible from all points of the whole and will look out towards them all.

Goethe's diary, 1800:

> 2 November. Early morning worked on *Faust* . . . In the afternoon continued work on *Faust*. – 3 November. Early morning worked on *Faust*. – 5 November. Worked on *Faust*. – 6 November. Worked on *Faust*. – 7 November. Worked on *Faust*. – 8 November. Early morning worked on *Faust*.

Goethe's diary, 1801:

> 8 February. Early morning worked on *Faust*. – 9 February.

Evening worked on *Faust*. [Then many such entries until 7 April 1801.]

Goethe to Schiller, 11 March 1801:

With *Faust* I make gentle progress. Though I do only a little each day, I strive to keep up my sense of it and my feeling for it.

Schiller to Goethe, Jena, 16 March 1801:

I wish you the best of luck as you progress with *Faust*. There are no words to express how keenly the philosophers here look forward to its appearance.

Goethe to Schiller, 18 March 1801:

I have not exactly come to a standstill with *Faust*, though my progress lately has been feeble. But since the philosophers are curious to see this work, I must of course make a greater effort.

Schiller to Cotta, 10 December 1801:

You ask after Goethe and his works ... He is too little master of his moods; his ponderousness makes him indecisive; and in his many amateur scientific pastimes he dissipates himself too greatly. I almost despair of his ever finishing *Faust*.

Goethe to Cotta, 30 September 1805 (Goethe was preparing to publish a big new edition of his works with Cotta; it would appear in 13 volumes between 1806 and 1810):

I am not quite decided what I should put into the fourth volume. If at all possible, I should like to see *Faust* there at once ... By when, at the latest, do you need the manuscript for Volume 4? That would help me plan things better.

Goethe's diary, 1806:

> 21 March. Began going through *Faust* with Riemer. – 24 March.
> *Faust* with Riemer. Last scene myself. – 25 March. *Faust* with
> Riemer. [And similar entries until] 21 April. *Faust* with Riemer,
> final revision. – 22 April. Went through *Faust* again myself. –
> 25 April. *Faust*, final arrangements for printing.

The manuscript was sent off, but the upheavals of war, 1806–7,
delayed production. Not until the Easter Fair of 1808 did *Faust,
Part I* appear, in Volume 8 of the *Works* published by Cotta.

Further Reading

English Translations of *Faust*, arranged chronologically

Anna Swanwick, in Bohn's Standard Library (*Part I*, 1850; *Part II*, 1879).

Theodore Martin (*Part I*, London, 1865; *Part II*, New York, 1886). Revised by W. H. Bruford, this was reissued in Everyman's Library (London, 1954).

Bayard Taylor (*Part I*, London and Boston, 1871; *Part II*, 1876).

Philip Wayne, Penguin Books (*Part I*, 1949; *Part II*, 1959).

Louis MacNeice and E. L. Stahl (both parts, abridged), Faber (1951; reissued 1965).

Barker Fairley (Toronto, 1970), a prose version.

Walter Arndt, edited by Cyrus Hamlin (New York, 1976; reissued 2001).

Randall Jarrell (*Part I*, 1976; reissued by Penguin in 2001).

Stuart Atkins (Boston, 1984).

David Luke, Oxford World's Classics (*Part I*, 1987; reissued 1998. *Part II*, 1994).

John R. Williams, Wordsworth Classics (*Part I* and *Urfaust*, Ware, 1999).

Books in English on Goethe's *Faust*

Butler, E. M., *The Fortunes of Faust* (Cambridge University Press, 1952; 1979).

Fairley, Barker, *Goethe's Faust: Six Essays* (Oxford University Press, 1953; 1965).

Gearey, John, *Goethe's Faust: The Making of Part One* (Yale University Press, New Haven, Conn., 1981).

Mason, Eudo C., *Goethe's Faust: Its Genesis and Purport* (University of California Press, Berkeley, 1967).

Williams, John R., *Goethe's Faust* (Allen & Unwin, London, 1987).

Books in English on Goethe and his Age

Boyle, Nicholas, *Goethe: The Poet and the Age*, vol. I: 1749–1790, vol. II: 1790–1803 (Oxford University Press, 1991 and 2000).

Bruford, W. H., *Germany in the Eighteenth Century* (Cambridge University Press, 1935; 1952).

—, *Culture and Society in Classical Weimar, 1775–1806* (Cambridge University Press, 1962).

Fairley, Barker, *A Study of Goethe* (Oxford University Press, 1947).

Friedenthal, Richard, *Goethe: His Life and Times* (Weidenfeld and Nicolson, London, 1965).

Gray, R. D., *Goethe: A Critical Introduction* (Cambridge University Press, 1967).

Lewes, G. H., *The Life and Works of Goethe* (London, 1855; reissued in Everyman's Library, 1949).

Lukács, Georg, *Goethe and his Age* (Merlin Press, London, 1968).

Reed, T. J., *The Classical Centre: Goethe and Weimar 1775–1832* (Oxford University Press, 1984).

—, *Goethe* (Past Masters Series, Oxford University Press, 1984).

Williams, John R., *The Life of Goethe: A Critical Biography* (Blackwell's, Oxford, 1998).

FAUST, PART I

DEDICATION

Unsteady shapes, who early in the past
Showed in my clouded sight, you approach again.
This time shall I attempt to hold you fast?
Am I disposed still to that fond temptation?
You rise around me out of haze and mist,
You press on me. So be it. Rule me then!
I feel your breeze and breath of magic start
The young self in me battering at my heart.

You bring the images of happy days with you
And many beloved shades arise,   10
First love and friendship rising with them too,
Like an old story caught before it dies;
The pain renews itself, lament again goes through
Life's labyrinthine errant ways
And names good people, cheated out of lovely
Hours by fortune, vanished ahead of me.

The souls I sang my first to cannot hear
What songs of mine come after. Far and wide,
Alas, my throng of friends are blown, and their
First answering voices with them died.   20
Now I perform to strangers as a stranger,
Even their approval makes my heart afraid
And those to whom my songs gave any joy
If they still live are scattered and astray.

And yearning, weaned away these many years,
Grips me for that grave quiet world of ghosts;
My verse waits on the undecided airs
And like a wind-harp sways and sounds and rests;
Cold visitation and a rush of tears,
30   Hardly at all the strict heart still resists,
What I possess looks far away to me,
Things vanished are becoming my reality.

PRELUDE IN THE THEATRE

[DIRECTOR, RESIDENT POET *and* COMIC.]

DIRECTOR

Friends, who so many times before
In need and woe have stood by me,
What do you think in Germany
The prospects for our business are?
I'd be well pleased if I could please the crowd.
They live and let live. I like them for that.
Our posts are in, our boards are laid
And everyone expects a treat.   40
Already in their seats with eyebrows raised
And all serene, they want to be amazed.
I know what keeps the general public satisfied
But till today was never so nonplussed.
Not that they're used to nothing but the best,
The trouble is: what quantities they read!
How shall we do it so that things are fresh and new
And meaningful and entertaining too?
For of course I like to see them stream in spate
To where we've set up shop and heave   50
In labour, as it were, and shove
For passage through the strait gate;
In broad daylight, not four o' clock,
Fighting their way with elbows to the till,
Like folk in famine at the baker's for a loaf, they will,
For a ticket, risk a broken neck.
This miracle on such a mix of humankind
Only a poet works. Work it today, my friend.

POET
    Don't speak to me of the motley and the many –
60   One look at them, the spirit abandons us.
    Hide all their mix and milling. Don't let me see.
    They pull us headlong where the current rushes.
    No, in a place of heavenly quiet confine me.
    Only there, for poets, pure joy flourishes
    Where love and friendship, quickening, nurturing,
    Deal our hearts a more than human blessing.

    Oh what the heart in that deep place taps into
    And shyly the lips try uttering aloud
    And goes awry and then, perhaps, comes true,
70   By the wild force of the moment is destroyed.
    Only after years, if it has struggled through,
    Appears a thing that's fully shaped and made.
    For the mere moment are the things that glitter
    And for posterity the things that matter.
COMIC
    Spare me posterity. Supposing I
    Took up discoursing on posterity
    Who then would keep the world we're in amused?
    But amused is what they want to be, and ought.
    Having a likely lad, I should have thought,
80   Present in person's not to be despised.
    Anyone easy in communication
    Won't let the people's moods embitter him.
    He wants big audiences for his presentation
    All the more certainly to move and shake them.
    Come now, show the world the way, be sure that when
    Imagination and all her choruses,
    Reason, Good Sense and Sentiment and Passion,
    Say their lines, the Fool also says his.
DIRECTOR
    Above all else, have plenty happening.
90   They come to watch, they want to see something.
    If lots is going on before their eyes
    And they're astounded while they stare

Then right away first prize
And popularity are yours for sure.
Only with masses can the masses be won,
In the end they all pick out what things they want.
Arrive with plenty and you'll give to each his own
And everyone goes home content.
Offer your piece in pieces here and now,
A stew like that's a simple job for you   100
And presentation is as easy as the invention.
And if you offer unity, why then
The audience unpicks it anyhow.

POET

You have no sense how poor such labour is.
No artist worth his salt would think it fit.
I see the way of every botcher is
Already the way you also go about it.

DIRECTOR

Though you reproach me you do not offend me.
A man who wants to work effectively
Should choose the tool that's best and stick to that.   110
It's soft wood you are splitting, don't forget.
Look who they are you're writing for!
One driven here by boredom and another
Comes bloated from excess of tablefare,
And, worst of all, among them there are those
Who come from reading the reviews.
Like folk distracted to a carnival they run this way
And only curiosity spurs them on.
The ladies fit themselves out for display
And act along, without remuneration.   120
To your sort musing on a mountain top
Why should a full house give delight?
Come down and see the customers close up:
Cold the one half and the other half red meat.
One after this play wants a night of gaming,
Another a wild night with the whores.
Poor fools the lot of you, why go on plaguing
The lovely Muses so in such a cause?

I tell you, give us more and more and more,
That way you'll never wander from the goal.
All you need try to do is muddle people,
To satisfy them is a hard labour . . .
Now what's troubling you, a pain, an ecstasy?

POET

Find someone else to shift for you! I won't.
You ask a poet on your account
To criminally throw away his highest right
And Nature's gift, the right of his humanity?
By what means does he agitate
All hearts and master every element?
By that accord that pulses from and then
Back into his heart enfolds the world again.
While Nature, turning indifferently, forces
Thread on the spindle without end,
And in our ears the untuned choruses
Of mixed and manifold existences contend,
Who'll measure off the unvarying succession
So that it lives and moves in rhythm? Who will call
Particular things to be a contribution
To the harmony of a festival of All?
Who mixes weather's rages with our own?
Who lends a heavy sense to sunset's reds?
Who flings the lovely blossom down
In spring wherever the beloved treads?
Who plaits the insignificant green of laurels
For a wreath to honour every sort of worth?
Who upholds Olympus and unites immortals?
Human power, in the poet bodied forth.

COMIC

Make use of it, this sweet ability,
And go about the work of poetry
The way we go about a love affair.
Chance meeting; feeling; rooting there;
Little by little two plait into one;
Happiness waxes, then comes tribulation;
We feel ecstatic, we feel doleful,

Before you know it, it's a novel.
Let's stage a show like that! Plunge fully in,
Both hands, in the abundant life of men and women!
All live this life, by most unrealized,
And always interesting wherever seized.
In motley images not much that's clear,   170
A little light of truth in plenteous error,
That way we brew the best drink of them all
That quickens everyone and edifies as well.
The loveliest bloom of youth will pack
The house and hark for revelation
And every tender heart will suck
A melancholic sustenance from your creation.
Exciting one and then another part
Each sees what he or she has most at heart.
Equally ready at that age to laugh or cry   180
They admire panache, still love the world of seeming.
Those who are finished you can never satisfy
But you'll have thanks from those who are still becoming.

POET

Then give me also back the time
When I myself was still becoming,
When from an ever-quickening spring
Unstoppably the poems came,
When mists concealed the world from me
And buds still promised miracles
And wealth and myriad variety   190
Of flowers were mine in all the dells.
I had nothing then, and yet enough:
The drive for truth and pleasure in illusions.
Give me unbridled the old compulsions,
Deep happiness and all its complement of pain,
The force of hate, the power of love,
Oh give me back my youth again!

COMIC

Youth, my dear friend, is a thing you need
When enemies oblige you to a fight;
When girls, superlatively sweet,   200

Storm you and will not be denied;
Or when you race and see the finish
And laurels at a breathless distance still;
Or when you dance like a whirling dervish
Then pass the nights in scoff and swill.
Friend, at your age it is your duty
To practise the familiar craft
Courageously and gracefully
And set the goals yourself and waft
210 Towards them in a pleasant mazy way,
For which we shall esteem you no whit less.
Old age doesn't make us childish, as they say,
It finds the true surviving child in us.

DIRECTOR

You've sent enough words to and fro.
Finally let me see some deeds as well.
Time spent on turning compliments can go
Instead on doing something useful.
What use is talk of being in the mood?
The mood will never choose a ditherer.
220 You say you're poets, do you? Good,
Tell poetry what her orders are.
You know what's wanted here: a long
And noisy draught of something strong.
Brew this for me and brew it now,
Not done today it won't be there tomorrow.
Don't let go by unused a single day,
Let Resolution seize the Possible
Bravely by the forelock right away.
When possibilities are seized and made to stay
230 The wish to shape them's irresistible.

In German theatres, as you know,
We give whatever we like a try.
Therefore no need to stint me now
On backdrops or machinery.
Deploy the bigger light of heaven and the less;
Be prodigal, by all means, with the stars.

Fire and flood we have and copious
Birds and beasts and gulphs and rocky tors.
Within the girdle of these walls confined
Pace out Creation's whole round   240
And with a measured haste propel
Yourselves from heaven through the world to hell.

PROLOGUE IN HEAVEN

[THE LORD, *the Heavenly Hosts. Later* MEPHISTO-
PHELES. *The three Archangels come forward.*]

RAPHAEL

As always still the day-star vies
In music with his brother spheres
And with the gait of thunder goes
His resonant determined course.
Watching the sun, unfathomable,
The angels wax in energy;
The high works, unimaginable,
250   Are glorious now as their first day.

GABRIEL

And fast, beyond imagining fast,
The splendours of the earth rotate,
And paradisal brightness must
Swap with deep and dreadful night;
The sea, wideflowing, lifts in spray
Against the deep cliff's rocky base
And rocks and sea are borne away
Fast in the spheres' eternal race.

MICHAEL

And roaring storms contend again
260   From land to sea, from sea to land
And couple up a furious chain
Of deepest workings all around.
And flames of lightning prepare
A wasteland in the thunder's way;

But we, your couriers, Lord, admire
The gentle changings of your day.

ALL THREE

The angels wax in energy
At your high works that here and now
Are glorious still as their first day
And nobody can fathom you.   270

MEPHISTO

Since, Lord, you join our company again
And ask how all things in our circle do
And used to like to see me, on occasion,
You find me here among the servants too.
Forgive me, I can't lift my language high enough
And will be sneered at here for that no doubt.
Pathos from me would surely make you laugh
Were laughter not a thing you've learned to do without.
The suns and planets are no theme for me.
How human beings torment themselves, that's all I see.   280
Earth's little god keeps true to type. He was
An oddity the first day and still is.
Somewhat his life would be in better plight
Had you not given him the shine of heaven's light.
He calls it reason and uses it
Only to be more bestial than any beast.
He seems – your Grace won't mind my saying so –
Like one of those long-legged grasshoppers who
Spring in the air and fly, but not for long,
And back in the grass then sing the same old song.   290
If only he would bide quiet in the grass!
Not poke his nose in every mess.

THE LORD

Do you have nothing else to say to me?
And never come but finding fault always?
Never a thing on earth gives you content?

MEPHISTO

I find things there, as ever, bad as bad could be.
I pity the poor creatures in the misery of their days,

Can scarcely bring myself to augment their torment.

THE LORD

Do you know Faustus?

MEPHISTO

                              Doctor?

THE LORD

                                        And my servant.

MEPHISTO

300   Indeed! His way of serving you is odd.
       His meat and drink are not the earthly sort.
       The ferment in him drives him ever further,
       He's half aware that he is raving mad,
       From heaven he wants the fairest star
       And from the earth then every highest pleasure
       And all things near and all things far
       Can't satisfy his foolish deeply agitated heart.

THE LORD

       What if he serves me in confusion now?
       Soon I shall lead him into clarity.
310   A gardener knows the leafing nursling tree
       With bloom and fruit will grace the years that follow.

MEPHISTO

       What do you wager? Lord, allow me
       Gently to lead him where I will,
       I promise you that you will lose him still.

THE LORD

       While he's alive on earth it shall
       Be not forbidden you. So long
       As human beings strive, they will go wrong.

MEPHISTO

       My thanks for that. For with the dead
       My wish to mix was never very strong.
320   I love the chubby cheeks, the rosy red;
       On days when corpses call I don't receive.
       Like any cat, I like my mice alive.

THE LORD

       Very well. Let it be left to you.
       Divert this spirit from his spring and source,

Grasp him, if you are able to,
And lead him with you on your downward course,
And stand ashamed when you are forced to recognize
A good man, though impelled in darkness, yet
Is well aware of what the right way is.

MEPHISTO
Good. We shan't be long about it.   330
I've no anxiety about my bet.
When I arrive at where I'm aiming at
Allow me then to shout my triumph out.
He shall eat dust and do so with delight
Like Cousin Serpent, of such good repute.

THE LORD
In that also I leave you free.
I never hated such as you.
Of all the spirits who say no
The rogue is the least burdensome to me.
Because man's energies flag all too easily   340
And peace and quiet are soon his sole ambition
I like to make the devil his companion
To prick and work and be a mover willy-nilly. –
But you, the gods' true sons, enjoy
The living beauty in abundance, by
The life forever working, ever new
Be sweetly wrapped around and lovingly confined
And shapes that hover wavering by you
Let them be steadied in a lasting mind.
      [*The heavens close, the Archangels disperse.*]

MEPHISTO [*alone*]
I like to see the old man now and then.   350
I work at good relations all I can.
In such a personage it is more than civil
To talk so humanly with the very devil.

THE FIRST PART OF
THE TRAGEDY

Night

[*A narrow and high-vaulted Gothic room.* FAUST *restless at his desk.*]

FAUST

Alas, I've studied Philosophy,
The Law and Physic and also,
More's the pity, Divinity
With ardent effort, through and through
And here I am, about as wise
Today, poor fool, as I ever was.
360   My title is Master, Doctor even
And up the hill and down again
Nearly ten years wherever I please
I've led my pupils by the nose –
And see what we can know is: naught.
When I knew this it seared my heart.
True, I know more than all the dimwits,
The doctors, masters, clerks and prelates.
I'm not tormented by doubt and scruple,
I'm not afraid of Hell and the Devil,
370   But all my joy has left me too,
I know that it's nothing good I know,
I know that what I teach won't mend
The minds and the manners of humankind.
I've neither goods nor gold and neither
Honour in the world nor any splendour.
A dog wouldn't live like this. So I

Have given myself to necromancy
To hear the mouths of ghosts disclose
In power some of their mysteries
And never again, in the sweat of my brow,   380
To speak of things I do not know
But see what in its innermost
Gathers the world and holds it fast,
Spy all the working and the seed,
The power – and quit the wordy trade.

O full moonlight, would that this were
Your last sight of my torment here!
So many midnights I have watched
You wax as though my watching fetched
You hither to lift above me, chained   390
To print and script, oh my sad friend
Could I but walk the mountains, high
In your beloved light, could I
Hover at mountain caves with ghosts,
Weave in the meadows in your mists,
Slough off the dross of knowing and in
Your dew bathe myself well again.

Stuck in the dungeon am I still?
Airless, cursèd hole-in-the-wall
Where even the lovely daylight shines
Muddily through the painted panes!   400
Confined behind the mounds of tomes
That dust shrouds and the worms eat at;
From floor to ceiling by reams and reams
Of sooty papers hedged about;
And circled in by jars and boxes
And instruments jam-packing it,
Ancestral lumber cramming it,
That is your world! What a world it is!

And you still wonder why your heart   410
In panic clenches tight in you?

Why ills you cannot fathom thwart
The starts of any life in you?
Instead of living Nature here
That Man was made within by God
Round you in reek and moulder are
Beasts' skeletons and bones of the dead.

Escape! Into a wider land!
And this book of the secrets by
420   Nostradamus's own hand
Be all your guide and company!
Knowing the starry courses then
Nature then your only tutor
In power your soul will lift and open
One spirit speaking with another.
The dry mind pondering here
Explains the holy signs vainly.
Oh, spirits you are hovering near,
If you can hear me, answer me.
   [*He opens the book and sees the Sign of the Macrocosm.*]
430   Oh what sharp pleasure at the sight of this
Flows at once through each and every sense.
I feel a young and holy happiness
Of life run glowing fresh through nerves and veins.
These signs, were they inscribed here by a god?
They make the turmoil in me still
And my impoverished heart joyful
And have mysteriously led
The powers of Nature all around me to unveil.
Am I a god? I have such light!
440   Before my viewing soul in these
Pure characters Nature, the worker, lies.
Now what the wise man says I grasp aright:
'The world of the spirits is not shut up,
Your mind is closed, your heart is dead.
Learner, be bold, arise and dip
Your earthly breast in daybreak's red.'
   [*He contemplates the Sign.*]

How everything into wholeness weaves,
Each in the other works and lives!
The climbing and descending powers of heaven!
The golden buckets in a chain!   450
Blessings on sweet wings fall,
Heaven enters earth and all
In harmony sounds through the All.

What theatre! Oh, but nothing more.
Where can I grasp you, never-ending Nature?
Breasts, where? You founts of all of life,
That earth and heaven hang upon with love
And where the parched soul craves to be,
You flow, you give to drink, but not to me.
    [*In vexation he turns the pages and sees the Sign of the
    Earth Spirit.*]
How different on me is the working of this sign!   460
Earth Spirit, you are nearer me.
I feel a lift of energy
And warming in me like new wine.
I feel the nerve to broach the world now
And bear it all, earth's joy, earth's sorrow,
And be a swaggering fighter in the tempest
And in the splintering wreck stand fast.
Clouds over me,
Moon hides her light,
The lamp is lost   470
In vapours, round my head
Red lightnings zig-zag, from the vaulting
Cold precipitates
And seizes hold of me!
Spirit I beg for, now I feel you hovering.
Unveil yourself!
Oh, in my heart such tearing
And all my senses boiling
Towards new feelings!
I feel my heart entirely given up to you.   480
You must! You must! Though it cost my life to do.

[*He seizes the book and in secret language utters the Spirit's sign. There is a flash of reddish flame, the* SPIRIT *appears in the flame.*]

SPIRIT

Who calls to me?

FAUST [*turning away*]

                You fill my eyes with fear.

SPIRIT

Powerfully you have tugged at me,
At my sphere of life sucked lengthily
And now –

FAUST

          Oh you are more than I can bear!

SPIRIT

With breaths you plead me into view,
To hear my voice, to see me face to face.
Your soul's hard pleading bending me to you
I have appeared. And now what piteous
490   Terror, *Übermensch*! Where is the soul's appeal?
Where is the heart that made a world and held
And harboured it within and swelled
On shocks of joy to be with us, the spirits, equal?
Whose sounding voice was it, who thrust
At me with all his force? Where are you, Faust?
Are you that man who now, touched by my breath,
Shakes to the living depths,
A timorous flinching worm?

FAUST

Before you, shape of flames, shall my nerve break?
500   I am that man, am Faust, I am your like.

SPIRIT

On life tides, in a storm
Of deeds I rise and fall,
Weave here and there
For birth, for burial,
A sea for ever,
A restless weaving,
A fiery living,

I work at the hurtling loom, I make
Of time God's living cloak.

FAUST

Looping the wide world round   510
How near you, busy spirit, I feel myself to be.

SPIRIT

You are like the spirit you can comprehend,
Not me.   [*Disappears.*]

FAUST [*collapsing*] Not you?
Who then?
After God's likeness and yet
Not even you?
    [*A knocking at the door.*]
Oh death! It is my *Famulus*.
So perishes my highest happiness.
That visions in such plenty must   520
Be interrupted by this creeper in the dust!
    [*Enter* WAGNER *in dressing-gown and nightcap, a lamp in
    his hand.* FAUST *turns to him impatiently.*]

WAGNER

Forgive me, I heard your declamation.
You were reading some Greek tragedy for sure.
This is an art I'd like to get on in
For nowadays it opens many a door.
Often enough I've heard it said
The actor could teach the preacher the way.

FAUST

If the preacher were an actor, yes he could,
And sometimes that might be so, I daresay.

WAGNER

Alas for the man who is banished to his study   530
And sees the world on Sundays, if at all,
And through a telescope, far distant, if at all.
How shall he guide the world by oratory?

FAUST

What you don't feel, you'll never get by chasing
Unless it presses from the soul
And with a primal deed of zestful pleasing

Puts every listener's heart in thrall.
Sit there forever, cut and paste,
Boil up a stew of others' hash
540 And puff alight what embers still subsist
Beneath your monticule of ash.
The children and the fools will cheer
If that's the sort of food you crave.
But heart to heart you'll never move
Unless your starting place is there.

WAGNER

Yet for the speaker delivery is all.
How far I lag behind I know full well.

FAUST

Look for your profit in an honest part.
Don't be the fool who comes on loudly sounding.
550 Good sense and proper understanding
Deliver themselves with very little art.
And if in earnest you have things to say
Will hunting after words be necessary?
Indeed your speeches that are so festooned
And glossy with the race's scraps and shives
Refresh as little as a foggy wind
Whistling in autumn through dead leaves.

WAGNER

God help us, art
Is long, and short our time alive.
560 Often while at the text I strive
I'm fearful for my head and heart.
How difficult it is to acquire
The means to climb up to the fountain-head
And very like, not halfway there,
Poor devils we drop down dead.

FAUST

Is parchment then the holy well
That drinking from you never thirst again?
It's not refreshment you have won
Unless it springs from your own soul.

WAGNER
  Forgive me, it delights and edifies   570
  To put oneself into the mind of times past,
  See how they thought who before us were wise
  And now how gloriously far we have come at last.

FAUST
  Far as the stars! Indeed we have come far!
  My friend, the ages that have passed, they are
  For us a book with seven seals
  And what you call the mind of the times,
  At bottom that mind is yours and it reveals
  Only its own reflection of the times
  And verily that is often a dismal sight   580
  And one to flee away from soon as seen:
  A lumber room, a rubbish bin
  Of melodramas of affairs of state
  And fine maxims for living fit,
  At best, to be mouthed by a marionette.

WAGNER
  But the world, the hearts and minds of humankind,
  Are subjects all men want to know about.

FAUST
  What they call knowing, that I do not doubt.
  But who dares speak his honest mind?
  The few who ever did know anything   590
  And were such fools they gave their hearts free rein
  And showed the mob what they had felt and seen,
  Death on the cross they got or death by burning.
  Now I beg you, friend, the night's far gone.
  We must break off our talk for now.

WAGNER
  I'd wake, and gladly, on and on and on
  To have such erudite debate with you.
  But tomorrow, being Easter Day,
  I'll ask you this and that still, if I may.
  I have applied myself to study with great zeal.   600
  True, I know much, but want to know it all.

                              [*Exit* WAGNER.]

FAUST [*alone*]
Why does not all hope flit from such a mind?
Adhering to the same stale stuff for ever
Greedily rooting after treasure
And finding worms and happy with the find.

How dare a human voice like his intrude
Where the spirits were abundant and I was in their midst?
And yet, alas, I owe you gratitude
Who are of all the earth's sons the least.
610   You tore me away from my despair
That threatened the undoing of my senses.
Oh seeing so giant a thing appear
I felt for certain my own dwarfishness.

Made in God's image, I who had supposed
Myself already near truth's mirror in eternity
And self-delighting in celestial shine and clarity
From kinship with the sons of the earth released,
More than the cherubim, by a large idea
Emboldening myself to flow through Nature's veins
620   Freely, strongly, and taste the life of heaven's
Gods as a creator, what a toll I pay:
A word of thunder dashes me away!

I cannot now presume to what you are.
Although I had the power to pull you here
I did not have the power to make you stay.
In that moment of blessedness
How small, how big I felt myself to be.
You thrust me back with harsh duress
Into the human lot, which is uncertainty.
630   Who can instruct me? What must I not do?
Shall I go where that longing leads?
Not just our sufferings, oh even our deeds
In life thwart our way through.

Stuff ever less fit thrusts itself upon
The spirit to shape the splendours it conceives.
Once having got to good things in our lives
The better are all deluding and delusion.
Our splendid feelings, givers of life to us,
Harden and die in the earthly press.
Where once imagination hopefully   640
Opened on bold wings towards eternity
A small room now is space enough for her
While in time's rapids happinesses founder.
Deep in the heart anxiety makes her nest,
In secret cradles her designs of pain
To and fro, never resting, mars all joy and rest,
She swaps her masks again and again,
Appears as house and home, as wife and child,
As fire or water, knife or poison.
You dread the things that never happen   650
And mourn as lost things you still hold.

I am not like the gods. That feeling has rooted fast.
I am like the worm that works the dust
And living in dust and by dust fed
Is crushed and buried by the walker's tread.

And these high walls here closing in on me
Their hundred sorted subjects, is that not dust?
All dust, the junk, the thousand kinds of vanity
In a world of moths by which I am oppressed?
The thing I lack, am I to find it in this place?   660
Shall I read in a thousand books that everywhere
The human being has been his own tormentor
And has been happy here and there and once or twice? –
O empty skull, what does your grinning say
But that your wits, confused once as mine are,
Sought daylight, lightness, and in twilight, heavy,
Eager for truth, went miserably in error?
How all these mechanisms jeer at me,

Wheel, cog, comb, roll of engine upon engine.
670 I stood at the gate, they were to be the key,
I had the allure, but could not enter in.
Mysterious in broad daylight, Nature
Will not permit the removing of her veil.
What she doesn't wish to open to your soul
Your screws and levers will not force from her.
Old gear I never had a use for, here
Only because my father did,
And on this desk old rolls of script sooted
By the dismal lamp's smoke year on year.
680 Far better had I squandered my small lot
Than burdened with it still sit here and sweat.
What you inherit from your fathers
Acquiring it, make sure you make it yours.
Things we don't use, heavily they burden us.
Only what the moment makes can the moment use.

But why do my glances fasten on that place?
Is that small bottle there a magnet for the eyes?
How everything sweetly suddenly clarifies
As though in a night wood moonlight found my face.

690 O vessel like none other, I salute you
And like a worshipper reach out to you.
I honour in you human wit and skill.
Essence of every blessed sleepy juice,
Extract of all the subtle powers that kill,
Favour your master with your virtues.
I see you, there is a lessening of pain,
I grasp you and the striving lulls,
The floodtide of the spirit falls.
I am turned out to face the open sea,
700 Now at my feet the mirroring waters shine,
Towards new shores a new day tempts me.

On easy wings a chariot of fire
Swoops down to me. I feel myself ready

To force a new way through the upper air
Towards new spheres of pure activity.
Bliss like the gods', a life at such a height,
Worm as you were, is that your due?
Yes, if I turn with a made-up mind and go
From earth's sweet sunlight
And be so bold and dare fling wide   710
The gates that all creep by in secret if they can.
Here it is time to prove with a deed
That a man may stand as tall as the heights of heaven
And not quake fearfully at that black hole
Of torments that the mind damns itself to
But strive towards the place of breakthrough
Round whose tight mouth flames the whole of hell,
Gaily resolve to take that stride
Even at the risk you melt into the void.

Pure crystal bowl, in many years   720
Never thought of, now let me lift you down
And from your ancient clothing slip you clean.
You shone at the joyful feastdays of our fathers,
When guests were solemn raised the cheerfulness
Among them, one to the next, passing between.
It was each drinker's task to commentate
In rhyme your copious wreath of images
And in one draught to drain the hollow dry.
I am reminded of many a youthful night.
Now I shan't hand you on to any next-in-line   730
Nor turn your art to be my wit's touchstone.
Here is a juice that makes drunk speedily.
With a brown flood it fills your hollow.
This drink, this last, my making, my own choosing,
With all my soul I do present it now
In high salute and ceremony to the morning.
    [*He raises the bowl to his lips. Pealing of bells and choirs
    singing.*]
CHOIR OF THE ANGELS
    Christ the Lord is risen again!

So to humans tried most sorely
By the ills that they are born with,
740   Ills that linger till they die,
Now this joy is given.

FAUST

The deep hum, the bright notes, why do they
Force down from my lips the lifted crystal?
Do these dull bells signal already
The first hour's worship in the Easter festival?
These choirs already sing their comfort-song
That once by angels' lips round the black grave was sung,
The certainty of the Covenant's renewal?

CHOIR OF THE WOMEN

Loyal to him
750   With spices we
Anointed him
And laid him down
And clothed him round
With linen, cleanly.
And now we find
Christ gone.

CHOIR OF THE ANGELS

Christ the Lord is risen again!
By his loving
On the grieving
760   On the testing and the proving
Comes salvation.

FAUST

Music of heaven, why do you come
With might and kindness looking for me in the dust?
Over there are soft humans: sound among them.
The good news comes to me, faith does not come.
Of all her children faith loves miracle best.
I dare not strive towards that zone
From where in music the glad tidings flow
And yet, accustomed since my boyhood, even now
770   The sound calls me to life again.
The kiss of heaven's love in that time past

Fell on me in the sabbath's solemn stillness,
And in the ample music of the bells, such promise!
And prayer then was a pleasure hot as lust.
And longing, past all understanding sweet,
Through field and forest drove me on and on.
In me, in the welter and the heat
Of tears, I felt new genesis happen.
This song started my boyhood's cheerful play,
The happiness set free in the festival of spring.   780
Now memory with a childish feeling
Keeps me from going the last grievous way.
Continue carolling, sweet songs of heaven,
I weep, I am for the earth again.

CHOIR OF THE DISCIPLES
    Now the buried man has risen
    Splendidly and regally,
    Risen alive, delighting in
    The act of moving on
    Close to where creation
    Works for joy. But we   790
    Suffering remain
    In the earth's bosom. Us
    He has left behind,
    Who were his, to pine.
    Oh, your happiness is,
    Master, grief to us.

CHOIR OF THE ANGELS
    Christ the Lord is risen from
    Corruption's womb.
    Now tear yourselves free
    Wholly and joyfully.   800
    Praise him by what you do,
    Prove your love, break
    The bread of fraternity.
    Travel far and wide and speak
    The happiness to come.
    The Master in all you do
    Is near, he is with you.

Outside the Town

[*All manner of people making their way out.*]

SOME APPRENTICES
Why that way? Where are you going to?

OTHERS
Hunters. And you?

FIRST GROUP
810   No, no, the Mill.

AN APPRENTICE
Better the Waterside. Take my advice.

ANOTHER
The way there's not so nice.

SECOND GROUP
And you?

A THIRD APPRENTICE
                    If they're going there, I will.

A FOURTH
Come up to Burgdorf. You're sure
Of the prettiest women there and the best beer
And first-class carryings-on.

A FIFTH
Not more shenanigan?
Twice already and you want the same again?
The place gives me the shivers. I'm steering clear.

SERVANT GIRL
820   No, no I'm going back.

SECOND SERVANT GIRL
We're bound to find him by the poplar tree.

FIRST SERVANT GIRL
What good will that do me?
He'll walk along with you
And only dance with you.
Will your good luck help me get what I lack?

SECOND
He won't be on his own today. The lad
With the curly hair will be there too, he said.

A STUDENT

    The way those girls walk! Seems to me
    We ought to keep them company.
    Strong beer, sharp stuff to smoke   830
    And a dressed-up girl, that's what I like.

BETTER-CLASS GIRL

    Look there, will you, it's a crying shame.
    Such pretty boys,
    Best company they could have if they chose
    And they run after girls like them.

SECOND STUDENT [*to the first*]

    Slow down. There's two back there
    Dressed up nicely.
    One of them lives next door to me
    And I like her.
    They're in no hurry. They'll be bound   840
    To take us with them in the end.

FIRST STUDENT

    No thanks. I don't want any difficulties.
    Quick or we'll lose the scent of the other two.
    Hands that use the broom on Saturdays
    Know best on Sundays what to do to you.

TOWNSMAN

    No, I don't like him, the new mayor.
    Now that he's it he's more barefaced by the day.
    And what's he doing for the town at all?
    Everything, is it not, is going downhill?
    Do as you're told, more than ever   850
    And more than ever, pay.

BEGGAR [*sings*]

      Gentlemen and lovely ladies
      So rosy-cheeked and in your Sunday best
      Be kind enough to cast your eyes
      On me, and lessen my distress.
      Don't leave me harping here without.
      Happy are only those who give.
      A day all people celebrate
      Be that a day when I receive.

ANOTHER TOWNSMAN

860   What I like best, Sundays and holidays,
      Is talk of war and of the din of war
      When over there, in Turkey, not near here,
      Nations are doling one another blows.
      You stand in the window, sup up once or twice
      And watch the gliding of the jolly ships downstream
      And in the evening in good humour you go home
      And say thanks be for peace and times of peace.

A THIRD

      Amen to that, neighbour. They're welcome
      To hack themselves to bits and everything
870   Can go to pot out there, so long as everything
      Stays how it always has been here at home.

OLD WOMAN [to the better-class girls]

      Young and pretty and dressed to kill
      What man won't you have at your beck and call?
      So why the airs? There's nothing more to do.
      What you are after I can get for you.

FIRST GIRL

      Agatha, come away. I've no desire
      To deal in public with a witch like her.
      True, on Saint Andrew's eve she did show me
      My future best beloved, bodily –

SECOND GIRL

880   She showed me mine too in her crystal ball,
      Bold and soldierly with several of that kind,
      And I've been looking everywhere around
      But still he hasn't come my way at all.

SOLDIERS

          The city walls,
          The high tower
          And girls that sneer
          And won't say yes
          It is for this
          Splendid spoil
890   The brave man toils.

We sound the trumpet,
We recruit
Perhaps for joy
Perhaps for grief.
That's the life!
We storm at it
And girls and cities
Have to give.
That's the spoil
For a brave man's toil,   900
The soldiers get it
And then they leave.
[*Enter* FAUST *and* WAGNER.]

FAUST

Life-giving looks of the sweet Spring
Have freed the streams and the river from their ice.
In the valley the happiness of hope is greening.
Old Man Winter, declining,
Into the harsh mountains shifts his biding-place
From where, retreated, he issues
Showers of icy grains that are powerless
In sweeps across the greening meadows.   910
But the sun will not tolerate any whiteness,
Everywhere things are shaping, things are striving,
And he wants colours to brighten their living
But on his patch flowers are in short supply
So he uses humans in their finery.
Turn on this rise. Look down
And back. See, from the town,
Out of the gate's dark hole,
The bright crowds pile.
All wish to be in the sun's warm regard.   920
They celebrate the risen Lord
For they are risen too: from homes
Low down, from close rooms,
From trade and labour's bonds,
The weight of roofs and gable-ends,
The squash and littleness of the streets

And the churches' venerable night
They are all brought into the light.
Look, only look how the quick crowd beats
930   A way through fields and plots
And how the river agitates
Along, across it, numerous cheerful boats
And there, overladen, hardly buoyant,
That last craft pulls away.
Even on the mountain paths, distant,
We glimpse some bright array.
I hear the villages' unholy row,
The true heaven of the people is here and now,
Contenting big and small, a noisy glee.
940   Here I am human, am allowed to be.

WAGNER
To take a walk with you, sir, is
An honour and a boon
But this is not a way I'd stray alone
Being, as I am, no friend of coarsenesses.
Fiddling, screaming, skittling
To my ears are detestable.
They rampage as if ridden by the devil
And call it being joyful, call it singing.

COUNTRY PEOPLE [*under the linden tree, dancing and*
          singing]
The shepherd dolled up for the dance,
950   Bright jacket, ribbons, flowery hat,
What's nattier than that?
The dancers scrummed around the tree
Like Bedlam on a holiday.
Hey diddle-dee!
Hey diddle-diddle-dee!
The fiddlestick was busy.

He hurried up to join the fun,
And accidentally, elbowing in,
He jabbed a lively girl but she
960   Faced and asked him haughtily

Was that your funny bone?
Hey diddle-dee!
Hey-diddle-diddle-dee!
Don't play that game with me.

But fast around the tree they went
Clockwise and then back again
And all the girls' skirts flew.
Soon they were red, soon they were warm,
They took a breather arm in arm,
Hey-diddle-dee!   970
Hey-diddle-diddle-dee!
And hip against elbow.

And don't be taking liberties,
So many make girls promises
And all their talk's a trick.
But he persuaded her aside
From under the linden where they cried
Hey-diddle-dee!
Hey-diddle-diddle-dee!
And plied the fiddlestick.   980

OLD COUNTRYMAN
   Sir, it is a courtesy
You do us being here today,
Here where all the people press.
A man so learned going his way.
Do more. Accept our finest bowl
That we with drink have freshly filled.
I offer it and wish aloud
That more than just your thirst be stilled.
May every drop of it increase
The number of your mortal days.   990

FAUST
   For this refreshment I give you all
Return of thanks and wish you well.
   [*The people gather round him.*]

OLD COUNTRYMAN
   Truly, it is meet and right
   That you appear this day when all are glad.
   You always had our good in mind
   In the past when days were bad.
   Many are standing here alive
   Because your father at the last
   Snatched them from the fever's fire and rage
1000   And set a limit on the pest.
   And you yourself, a young man then,
   Visited every hospital.
   Many a corpse was carried away
   But you, emerging, had no ill.
   You had hard trials and you came through.
   For helping us, heaven helped you.

ALL
   Good health to the tried and tested man!
   Long may he help and help again.

FAUST
   Bow down to Him who from above
1010   Gives help and teaches us to give.

               [He goes on his way with WAGNER.]

WAGNER
   What, in your greatness, must your feelings be
   As you receive this crowd's homage!
   Happy the man of parts when they
   Procure him such advantage.
   The father shows you to his boy,
   And all enquire and hurry up and jostle,
   The fiddle halts, the dance stands still,
   And where you walk they line the way,
   And fling their caps in the air. Why they
1020   Are nearly on their knees as though
   The host were being carried through.

FAUST
   Only a few steps higher, to that stone.
   Now we can rest from walking. Here,
   Pensive, I often sat alone

Tormenting myself with fasting and with prayer.
Rich in hope, firm in faith, by violence
Of weeping, sighing, wringing hands I thought
From the Lord of Heaven I could extort
The ending of that pestilence.
Like scorn I hear the people's cheering now.   1030
If you could read my heart you'd know
How little on such fame
The father and the son have any claim.
My father was an honourable man
Who pondered Nature's sacred nexus
Honestly but after his own fashion,
Occluded, quirky and laborious.
With adepts for companions
He shut himself in the black laboratory
And from interminable prescriptions   1040
Poured together what was contrary.
There a Scarlet Lion, a bold suitor,
He married to the Lily in a lukewarm bath
And over an open flame tormented both
To quit one bridal chamber for another.
If in the glass, brightly coloured,
Thereupon the Young Queen showed
That was the medicine, the patients died
And no one asked, were any cured?
So with our hellish syrups we ran   1050
Through these hills and valleys with more virulence
By far than the very pestilence.
I myself gave thousands the poison.
They wasted. I have lived to listen to
The insolent murderers' *laudatio*.

WAGNER

Why should that trouble you? Surely
When the arts are handed on to him
It is sufficient that the good man practise them
Punctiliously and conscientiously?
You, as a young man, honouring your father   1060
Are glad to have what comes to you from him.

If, as a grown man, you increase that sum,
Your son will push his pebble even further.

FAUST

I call him happy who still hopes to rise
To the surface in this sea of error.
The very things we don't know, we could use
And what we do know we have no use for.
But let us not wither the good and beauty
Of this hour by the mind's sad cast.

1070   See how the little houses placed in greenery
Shine in the fires of sunset. This is the last
Of the life of the day. The sun is shifting, giving
And hurrying to further new life over there.
Oh, I want wings to lift me up for striving
After, always after, from the ground here.
In the eternal beam of evening
I'd see the still world under me and every fold
Of earth at peace, the hilltops shining,
The silver beck flowing into streams of gold.

1080   The gashed and savage mountains cannot stop
Flight like that, a god's, the eyes
Are amazed already as the sea's
Warmed inlets open up.
There, so it seems, the god sinks finally.
But it wakes new appetite.
I hurry on, to sup his lasting light,
Night at my back, the day ahead of me,
The heavens above me and the waves below.
A fine dream. The sun escapes meanwhile.

1090   Oh we want wings for the body to sail
With the spirit's wings, and don't know how.
And yet by nature we are driven to
Ride on the feeling higher and further still
When above our heads, lost in the roomy blue,
Larks into loud song overspill
And when over evergreens
On abrupt cliffs we see the eagle come
Spread-winged freeriding down, and cranes

Over lakes and flatlands heading home.

WAGNER

I have had strange ideas of my own   1100
Often, but no impulse like yours. One soon
Finds fields and woodland wearisome.
I'll never envy birds their wings. The flight
From page to page and tome to tome
On the wings of the mind is my delight.
The winter nights are sweet then, through and through
The body warms with blissful life. Unroll
Some venerable parchment and the whole
Of heaven comes down to earth for you.

FAUST

You only know the one impulse. Oh may   1110
The other never come into your ken.
Alas, I house two souls in me
And each from each wants separation.
With love, with rough delight, keenly the one
Holds to the earth, with battening organs, fast.
The other by main force lifts from the dust
Into the realms of the high ancestry.
If there are spirits in the air between
Heaven and earth that rule and weave,
Out of the golden haziness come down   1120
And carry me where a bright life comes alive!
Oh, if I had a magic cloak that bore
The wearer into foreign lands I'd not
For the costliest be bartered out of it
No, not for the mantle kings wear.

WAGNER

Do not call up that well-known company
That spread in streams through the circumambient haze
From the earth's four quarters in a thousand ways
Devising perils on humanity.
Sharp spirit-fangs and arrow-pointed tongues   1130
Arrive from the north, assailing you and from
The east the desiccators come
That get their nourishment feeding on your lungs,

And when the south looses around your brows
Out of the desert fire on fire,
Then the swarming west refreshes you before
Drowning you with all your fields and meadows.
They hearken willingly, they harm with glee
And, glad to fool us, willingly obey.
1140 They pose as heaven's emissaries,
Murmur like angels while they tell their lies.
But let us go. Already the world is grey,
The air cooling, mist coming down. Truly
At nightfall then we value home. But why
Do you stand there struck? What is it you see?
What is it in the twilight has you spellbound?

FAUST
That black dog loose in the seed and stubble ground.

WAGNER
I saw him long since. He seemed nothing to me.

FAUST
Look again. What do you take the beast to be?

WAGNER
1150 A poodle who, after his fashion,
Frets himself on his master's trail.

FAUST
Do you not see how, in a wide spiral,
He races around us, closing in?
And after him, if I am not mistaken,
He tows a wake of fire.

WAGNER
All I see is a black poodle. For sure,
With you this is some optical illusion.

FAUST
He seems to be drawing nooses round our feet
Magically softly, for a future bond.

WAGNER
1160 I see him in his capering hesitate
Fearful it's strangers not his master he has found.

FAUST
The circle shrinks. Now he is near.

WAGNER

And see, we have a dog and not a spectre here.
He growls and wonders, lies down flat.
He wags his tail. All dogs behave like that.

FAUST

Come then and keep us company.

WAGNER

The beast has all the poodle's idiocy.
Stand still, he'll wait at your beck and call,
Speak to him, he will stretch up tall,
Leave something lying, he will bring it back   1170
And leap in the water for your walking stick.

FAUST

I'm sure you are right. I see no kind
Of spirit in him. All comes from being trained.

WAGNER

Rightly a well-trained dog enjoys
The good opinion even of the wise.
Yes, he deserves your favour to the full,
Being your students' excellent disciple.

> *[They go back through the gate into the town.]*

Faust's Study (I)

> *[FAUST enters with the poodle.]*

FAUST

I've left the fields and meadows. While
A deep night covers them it rouses
The sacred and the better soul   1180
With thrills of wishful terror in us.
Now the wild impulses are quietened
And all unbridled action too.
The love of humankind is quickened
Now and the love of God also.

Be still, poodle, stop running to and fro.
Why are you snuffling at the threshold here?
Lie down behind the stove, will you.
I've given you my best cushion there.
1190   When we were out, on the hilly way,
It entertained us, how you leapt and ran.
Accept from me now hospitality
And be a welcome guest, a quiet one.

Oh when for us, confined, apart,
Again the friendly lamplight burns
Within as well, in any heart
That knows itself, the light returns.
Reason begins to speak again
And hope again begins to flower.
1200   We long for the living waters then,
For the springs of life, oh to be there!

Stop growling, poodle. Animal noise
Sorts ill with the heavenly harmonies
Now taking possession of all my soul.
We are well used to men
Scoffing at what's beyond their ken,
Grumbling at the good and the beautiful,
Which often for them are wearisome.
Do dogs by growling do the same?

1210   But oh, already, however hard I will,
I feel my spring of satisfaction fail.
Why must the waters give out so soon
And leave us lying in drought again?
That has been my lot, so often.
But there's a way to make good the want:
We learn to value what's beyond the earth,
We yearn for revelation
And that shines best and loveliest forth
From the New Testament.
1220   I am impelled to broach the text and bring

With heart and soul
The holy original
Across into my beloved German tongue.
   [*He opens a volume and sets to.*]
It is written: 'In the beginning was the *Word*.'
I baulk at that. Who'll help me onward?
I cannot rate the *word* so highly,
I must translate it differently.
Enlightened by the spirit I see written
'In the beginning there was *Thought*.' Think again
And hard at this first verse. Maybe   1230
Your pen was over hasty.
Is *thought* the maker and the doer?
'In the beginning' – so it ought to read – 'was *Power*.'
I write this down, but even as I do
I hear a warning that I cannot leave it so.
The spirit helps. Now I decide
And write with confidence: 'In the beginning was the *Deed*'!

If you and I are to room together,
Poodle, you must cease
Howling and barking. I can't bear   1240
Anyone in my living space
Making a din like that.
One of the two of us must quit
This cell. Though I don't like to show
A guest the door, I show it now
Wide open. Off you go.
But what do I see?
Can this be happening naturally?
Is it a wraith or a real thing?
My poodle broadening and lengthening!   1250
From being a dog he rises
In furious metamorphosis.
What ghoul did I bring home? He has
The look of a hippopotamus
With frightful jaws and eyes of fire.
Oh I know you for sure.

On such half-breeds of hell
The Key of Solomon works well.

SPIRITS [*in the passage outside*]
There's one nabbed in there!
1260   Stay outside, beware!
One of hell's canniest
Quakes like a fox caught fast.
But heed!
Flit to and fro
And high and low
And he will be freed.
You who have help to give
Don't leave him captive.
He has done all of us
1270   Many a kindness.

FAUST
First to make the beast appear
I speak the spell of the four:
Salamander, burn.
Undine, twist and turn.
Sylph, to thin air.
Goblin, to labour.
Who has not the lore
Of the elements, all
Their power,
1280   Their nature,
The spirits are never
At his beck and call.
Vanish in flames,
Salamander!
Mix with the rushing streams,
Undine!
Dazzle as a meteor,
Sylph!
Bring help to the house,
1290   Incubus! Incubus!
Make an end, show yourself!

The beast does not harbour
Any of the four.
He lies there calmly and grins at me.
So far I have done him no injury.
I'll conjure you
Harder now.
   Have you fled here,
   Thing, from hell fire?
   Then look on this sign   1300
   To which all Hell's
   Black crowds bow down.
See how he bristles, how he swells!
   Creature, outcast,
   Can you read the One
   From no seed sprung,
   Never expressed,
   Transpierced by wrong
   And streaming down the skies of heaven?
Behind the stove, where it was sent,   1310
It swells up like an elephant
Filling all the room and willing
Itself to a mist.
Don't rise to the ceiling!
Lie down at your master's feet.
You see this is no idle threat,
I'll sear you with a holy heat.
Don't wait
For the triply burning light.
Don't wait   1320
To feel the worst that I can do.
   [*As the vapours subside* MEPHISTOPHELES, *dressed like
   a travelling scholar, steps forward from behind the
   stove.*]

MEPHISTO
   Why all the noise? What may we do for you?

FAUST
   So that was under the poodle's skin!

A travelling scholar? The outcome makes me laugh.

MEPHISTO

I raise my hat to the learned gentleman.
You made me sweat more than enough.

FAUST

What are you called?

MEPHISTO

That seems a little question
For you who so despise the Word and strive
Far beyond appearance and illusion
1330   Where living things are most deeply alive.

FAUST

With your sort we may usually assume
The nature from the name;
In which it is all too clear
When the name is Lord of the Flies, Destroyer, Liar.
So then, who are you?

MEPHISTO

A part of the power who
Wills evil always but always works the good.

FAUST

How shall these riddling words be understood?

MEPHISTO

I am the spirit of always saying no
And I am right, for everything that comes to life
1340   Is fit to perish. So
Better if nothing ever came to life.
Thus everything that you call sin,
Destruction – in brief,
Evil – is the element I'm at home in.

FAUST

You call yourself a part but stand before me whole?

MEPHISTO

I speak the modest truth. Admittedly
That little world of fools, humanity,
Does like to think itself a whole –
I'm part of the part that in the beginning was all,

Part of the dark that gave birth to the light,   1350
Proud light that now disputes with Mother Night
Her old status and space and never will
Prevail however hard it strives because
It clings to bodies,
Streams with bodies, makes them beautiful,
A body thwarts it in its onward course
And so, I hope, before much longer
With the bodies light too will go under.

FAUST

Now I know what your noble duties are!
Unable on the large scale to annihilate a thing   1360
You make a start now on the small.

MEPHISTO

                    Aware
I don't do much, so doing.
The thing opposing Nothingness,
The something, this crass world, though I
Have striven against it officiously
I never have had any success
With waves and tempest, quake and flame –
The sea and the land go on the same.
And as for that damned stuff, the brood of man and beast,
They can't be damaged in the least.   1370
However many I inter
There's always fresh new blood in circulation.
It drives you mad how it goes on and on.
Out of the earth, the air, the water,
Seeds in thousands wriggle free
In the dry, the wet, the warm, the cold.
Had I not laid a claim on flame, what would
There be exclusively for me?

FAUST

So you oppose to the ever agile
Powers that make and heal   1380
The cold fist of the devil
Clenched in a vain illwill.

But then, strange son of chaos,
What else could you ever do?

MEPHISTO

Indeed, we shall give some thought to this.
More on it anon. You will permit
Me now to take my leave of you?

FAUST

I don't see why you need my yes or no.
Now that you and I have met
1390   Visit me when you feel like it.
Here is the window, here is the door,
And there's a chimney too at your disposal.

MEPHISTO

Let me confess that one small obstacle
Prevents my walking out of here.
The witch's foot on your threshold . . .

FAUST

The pentagram pains you? Well then,
Son of Hell, tell me, if you are held
Spellbound by that, how was it you got in?
What could have hoodwinked such a spirit?

MEPHISTO

1400   Look closely. It is not drawn tight.
One of the corners, that one pointing out,
Does, you will notice, gape a bit.

FAUST

That was a lucky accident and it
Makes you my prisoner. Am I right?
I never aimed at this success!

MEPHISTO

The poodle, when he sprang in, did not notice.
But now the matter has a different face.
The devil cannot leave the house.

FAUST

But what about the window? Exit there.

MEPHISTO

1410   It is a law on devils and ghosts that where
They slipped in there they must slip out.

Only for entry do we have a choice.

FAUST

So even hell is a regulated state?
That pleases me. A man might enter into
A pact with you and yours in some security?

MEPHISTO

What we promise, you will enjoy freely
And not one jot of it be docked you.
But these are not things to abbreviate.
We must discuss them at some later date.
For now, with every last superlative,   1420
I beg that you will let me take my leave.

FAUST

No, no. Not yet a while. Stay till
You've told me things I'm curious to learn.

MEPHISTO

Release me now. Before long I'll return.
Then you can ask me all you will.

FAUST

But I did not come hunting you.
You ran into the snare yourself. The man
Who holds the devil should not let him go.
It is not likely he will capture him again.

MEPHISTO

If that's your wish then I shall stay   1430
And willingly keep you company
But on condition you allow me by
My arts to pass the time for you in some fit way.

FAUST

I shall be glad to see it. Try!
But let the art be of a pleasing kind.

MEPHISTO

Your senses will enjoy, my friend,
In this one hour far more
Than in a humdrum year entire.
What the gentle spirits sing you,
The lovely images they bring you   1440
Are not an empty magic play.

Your nose will be delighted,
Your taste buds sweetly treated,
And touching will be ecstasy.
It needs no preparation.
We are assembled. So begin!

SPIRITS

Let the dark vaulting
Vanish and through
Come the quickening,
1450   The friendly, the blue
Upper air.
Oh, if the dark
Clouds would clear,
Little stars sparkle
And milder suns
Come shining in.
The Sons of Heaven,
Ghostly beauty,
Bowing, swaying,
1460   Hover by
And a love, a longing
Follows them over.
The fluttering ribbons
On all they wear
Cover the countries,
Cover the greenery,
Where for their lives
Thoughtful lovers
Give themselves.
1470   Green on greenery,
A sprouting, twining,
Disburdened vines,
So vat and press
Are tumbled full
And frothing wines
Stream and trickle
Quick through precious
Stones and crystal

And leave the high land
Lifted behind 1480
And widen around
The greening hills
To lakes, for pleasure.
And the fowls of the air
Sup up delight
And make on wings
For the sun, on wings
For the bright isles
On the moving waters
Shimmying in light. 1490
And we listen there
To rejoicing choirs
And over the meadows
Watch the dancers
Strew their pleasures
Under open skies.
And some are climbing
Over the hills,
Others are swimming
The lakes and above 1500
Others are sailing
The air, and all
Into life, to the far off
Stars of love
Praising and blessed.

MEPHISTO
He sleeps. Well done, my gentle boys!
Your concert in the air has shut his eyes,
I'm in your debt for these loyal lullabies.
You are not yet the man to hold the devil fast!
Flit round him with sweet dream shapes, trick 1510
And sink him in the ocean of delusion.
But to crack this threshold's magic
A rat's teeth will be necessary.
Rats won't need much conjuring. One
Scuttles up already. He'll heed me.

The Lord of Rats, the Lord of Mice,
Of Flies and Frogs and Bugs and Lice
Commands you: show your face
And use your teeth on the threshold there.
1520   A dab of oil marks the place –
And here you come, hurry, scurry!
To work at once! I'm spellbound by
That salient front point of the star.
One more bite and then it's done.
Dream on, Faustus, until we meet again.

FAUST [*waking*]

Have I been tricked a second time?
Is this how the rush of spirits finishes?
That I am shown the devil by a lying dream
And a poodle vanishes?

Faust's Study (II)

[FAUST *and* MEPHISTOPHELES.]

FAUST

1530   A knock? Come in! Who is it plagues me now?

MEPHISTO

I do.

FAUST

Come in!

MEPHISTO

Say it a third time, will you?

FAUST

Come in then!

MEPHISTO

That's the spirit.
We shall, I hope, get on together.
To end your moping I am here
In a noble Junker's outfit,
In gold-trimmed red and over that
A cape of stiffened silk, my hat

Sports the rooster's feather,
And I wear a long sharp sword
And counsel you now, in a word,   1540
To attire yourself in like manner
And so, let off the leash and free,
Find out what life is like or might be.

FAUST

This narrow earth-life's pain will stay
In me whatever my attire.
I am too old to do nothing but play,
Too young to be without desire.
What can the world give me? Deny
Yourself! Do not enjoy!
That is the one and only song   1550
That, all of us, we ever hear
That hoarsely every single hour
Regales us with all our lives long.
Only with horror do I wake each day
And near to bitter weeping when I see
The day that in its course will not fulfil
One wish of mine, not one, but will
With selfish carping stunt
All pleasure even in presentiment
And with a thousand of life's idiocies thwart   1560
The energies of my heart.
Come nightfall, I am certain
To lie down with anxiety
And no rest will be given me then
But wild dreams frighten me.
The god indwelling in me causes
Deep turmoil innerly
But he, the lord of all my energies,
Can move not one thing outwardly.
So my existence is burdensome,   1570
Death to be wished, life loathsome.

MEPHISTO

Yet Death, the visitor, is never wholly welcome.

FAUST

I call him blessed whose head Death winds
Around with bloody laurels as the illumined
Victor or, at the hectic dancing's end,
Soon in a girl's embrace Death comes and finds.
Oh when the High Spirit came would I had sunk
Under his power, unsouled by the ecstasy!

MEPHISTO

And yet that night a certain somebody
1580   Left a brown juice undrunk.

FAUST

Spying, it seems, is your delight.

MEPHISTO

                                   Though not

Omniscient, I know a lot.

FAUST

By an old sweet music I was pulled
Then from my spirits' terrible throes.
It touched on happy times and told
My lingering childish feeling lies.
But now I curse all things that have
The soul in check by lure and illusion,
That banish her to this sad cave
1590   By powers of blinding and deception.
Cursed be every big idea
The mind puts on to hide in like a shell.
And cursed be all phenomena
That dupe the senses they assail.
Cursed be dreams and vain believing
That name and fame will never end.
Cursed be the blandishment of having
A wife and child, household and land.
Cursed be Mammon when for riches
1600   He urges us to recklessness
Or plumps the pillows under us
For pleasurable idleness.
I curse the kind juice of the grape,
I curse the best love gives, let fall

My curse on faith, my curse on hope –
And patience: curse that most of all!

CHORUS OF SPIRITS [*invisible*]

    Alas! Alas!
    You have destroyed
    The lovely world
    With a powerful fist,
    It falls, it falls to bits,   1610
    A demigod has smashed it.
    We carry
    The ruins across into nothingness
    And over the lost
    Beauty we grieve.
    Splendid among
    Earth's sons
    By your power
    Build the world again   1620
    In your heart build the world up again.
    Lighten
    Your mind and be
    Newly alive
    Whereupon
    New songs will be sung.

MEPHISTO

    Listen to these
    My little ones wise
    Beyond their years how they counsel you
    To enjoy and to do.   1630
    They wish to persuade
    You out of your solitude
    Where the senses and juices cannot run free
    Into the world at liberty.

    Give over idling with your ill.
    It gnaws your vitals like a vulture.
    In company, however bad, you'd feel
    As they are human so you are.
    Not that we mean

1640   To thrust you in among the hoi polloi.
I'm not one of the great, but I,
If you will join your steps with mine,
Through life then willingly
I'll fit myself to be
All yours, right here
I'll be your fellow wayfarer
And giving satisfaction
Your menial, your bondsman.

FAUST
And what's the quid pro quo?

MEPHISTO
1650   Before that's wanted much time will have passed.

FAUST
No, no, the devil is an egoist,
Not likely gratis, for rewards in heaven, to do
A thing in anyone else's interest.
Say clearly what the deal is. We bring
Some danger home by such a hiring.

MEPHISTO
I bind myself to serve you here
And non-stop do your bidding, tirelessly.
If and when our paths cross over there
You will do the same for me.

FAUST
1660   Over there is small concern of mine.
Once you have smashed this world to smithereens
The other may arise then if it will.
My joys well from this earth alone
And on my sufferings only this sun shines.
Once I can part from them let happen
Whatever wishes to and can.
On that subject I've heard my fill,
Whether in the future we still hate and love
And whether in those spheres still
1670   There's a below or an above.

MEPHISTO
In that mind you can risk it then.

Bind yourself: and in the coming days
With my arts I'll delight your eyes.
I'll give you things not seen by any human.

FAUST

Poor devil, what will you be giving?
Was a human being's spirit in its high striving
Ever comprehended by your sort?
But do you have food that leaves the eater hungry,
Red gold that cannot rest but runs apart
In the hand, quicksilvery,   1680
A game I lose at every time,
A girl who pillowed on my heart
Already eyes and contracts with my neighbour,
The enjoyment, like a god's, of lovely fame
That vanishes like a meteor?
Show me the fruit that rots before it's in the hand
And trees day after day greening again.

MEPHISTO

I'm not dismayed by any such demand.
I can oblige you richly in that line.
But also, my dear friend, there are times when   1690
A man might like to eat well at his ease.

FAUST

If ever I settle on a bed of ease
Let me be done for there and then.
If you, by lying flattery, can please
Me with myself and can impose,
By means of pleasure, upon my mind –
There and then let my days end.
I offer you this wager.

MEPHISTO

               Done!

FAUST

                    My hand!
If ever I shall tell the moment:
Bide here, you are so beautiful!   1700
Then you can fetter me and I'll
Go gladly to perdition that instant.

Then let the death-knell toll,
Of all your service then you're quit,
The clock can stop, the fingers fall
And time for me is past. So be it.

MEPHISTO
Give it due thought. We shan't forget.

FAUST
And you have every right not to forget.
But this is not an act of bad presumption.
1710   I am a slave as I am now,
Yours or who else's, all one.

MEPHISTO
Forthwith, at the doctoral feast today,
I shall fulfil my duties serving you.
But first: for life's or death's sake, if I may,
I'll ask you for a line or two.

FAUST
Pedant, you want the thing in writing, do you?
You never met a man whose word you'd trust?
Is it not enough that to the last
My spoken word will govern my days?
1720   See how the hurtling world in all its waters flees!
And shall a written promise hold me fast?
But this delusion is our given maxim
And few are willing to be rid of it.
Happy the man who keeps faith pure within him!
He pays whatever cost without regret.
But a parchment written and embossed
Is a spectre everybody fears.
Before it leaves the pen the word expires
And nothing counts but wax and vellum.
1730   Spirit of evil, which is it you want?
Bronze, marble, paper or parchment?
Shall I write with stylus, chisel, quill?
I offer you whatever's to your liking.

MEPHISTO
Why heat yourself with speechmaking

At once in that exaggerated fashion?
Any scrap of paper will do very well.
You sign your name with a little drop of blood.

FAUST

If that will give you satisfaction
The foolery, for all I care, can go ahead.

MEPHISTO

Blood is a quite particular juice.   1740

FAUST

Don't fear I won't keep to the here agreed.
For what I promise is indeed
The striving of all my energies.
I puffed myself too high. Your rung,
No higher, is where I belong.
The Great Spirit put me off below
Contempt, and Nature shuts me out.
The thread of thought is cut.
I sickened of all science long ago.
So in the deep of sensuality   1750
I'll quench my passions' heat.
Make me at once all kinds of wonder ready,
Still wrapped in magic, still to penetrate.
I'll ride the rush of time and chance
The switchback of occurrence,
And there let pain and pleasure,
Bad setback and success,
Swap as they will with one another.
A man must do the acts of restlessness.

MEPHISTO

No limit is set you and no measure,   1760
But titbits everywhere, if that's your pleasure.
Grab what you like as you flit by,
I wish you joy of it, whatever pleases you.
Only: don't dally, don't be coy.

FAUST

You heard me, joy is not the issue.
I give myself to frenzy, to pleasure that hurts most,

Hatred in love and setbacks that revive.
My heart, cured of the knowledge-drive,
Henceforth to all the sorrows will be host
1770   And what is dealt to all humanity
That I'll enjoy in my self's innermost,
Seize with my spirit the highest and the deepest
And heap all humans' weal and woe on me
And widen my own self to encompass theirs
So when they do, that self likewise founders.

MEPHISTO
Believe me who have chewed at this tough cud
For several thousand years: no human
Between the cradle and the grave has time enough
To digest the ancient sourdough.
1780   Believe me and my kin:
This whole is only for a god.
He dwells eternally in light,
Us he consigned to darkness, you
All you are fit for's day and night.

FAUST
But I want to.

MEPHISTO
                    I'm glad to know it.
But one thing bothers me. Since time
Is short and art is long you should,
I think, take some instruction.
Seek the society of a poet
1790   And let that gentleman's imagination run
And heap upon your honourable dome
Every noble quality:
The lion's bravery,
The deer's fleetfootedness,
The Italian's fiery blood,
Northern steadfastness.
Let him teach you how to marry
Being generous with being sly
And fall in love like a young man
1800   Warmly, impulsively, after a plan.

I wish some such person would come
My way. I'd call him Mr Microcosm.

FAUST

What am I then if I can never
Get the crown of the human race
After which all the senses chase?

MEPHISTO

You are in the end . . . the thing you are.
Pile wig on curly wig upon your pate
And sock on comic sock beneath your feet
You are the thing you are, still and for ever.

FAUST

I feel it: I have snatched in vain   1810
All the valuables of the human mind
To me and at the end when I sit down
No force in me that's new can be divined.
I am not by one hair's breadth higher,
To things that have no end I am no nearer.

MEPHISTO

The way you look at things, my friend
Is just the usual way they get looked at.
We need a cleverer way than that
Before life's pleasures end.
Hang it, of course my hands and feet   1820
And arse and head-piece are my own
But all the things I use for my delight
Surely as much are mine.
If I can get six horses with my cash
Do I not own their energy?
I run along and cut a manly dash
As though my legs were four and twenty.
Leave off brooding. Let us go
Into the wide world, you and I, pronto.
I tell you, the man who cogitates   1830
Is like a beast on dry heathland
Led round and round by evil sprites
And fine green pasture lying just beyond.

FAUST
  How shall we start?

MEPHISTO
                          By leaving here.
  What a place of torment this is, to be sure!
  Boring the young and yourself too,
  What sort of life is that? I ask you!
  Why plague yourself with thrashing straw?
  Let Colleague Fatty do it. Nor
1840 Is the best that it is possible to know
  Fit to be told the boys. Apropos
  I hear one in the corridor.

FAUST
  I cannot see him.

MEPHISTO
                          The poor thing
  Has waited a good while and must not go
  From here without some comforting.
  Give me your cap and gown. I'll be
  Deliciously well suited in this fancy dress.
    [*He disguises himself.*]
  Now leave the rest to my inventiveness.
  I want ten minutes or so. Make ready
1850 Meanwhile, will you, for the journey.

                                    [*Exit* FAUST.]

MEPHISTO [*in* FAUST's *long gown*]
  Go on, despise science and reason,
  Highest of all the powers that humans have,
  And only let the lying spirit give
  You strength in works of magic and illusion.
  Then without question you are mine –
  Fate's gift to him's a spirit always driving
  On and on, allowed free rein,
  And in its headlong striving
  It overleaps the joys of earthly living.
1860 I'll drag him through a wild existence
  Through flat want of significance,
  I'll see him dangling in it, fixing, cleaving

And meat and drink will hover over
The lips of his never-to-be-sated craving.
He'll beg for slaking and will get it never
And even were he not pawned to the devil
He'll go down to perdition still.

[*Enter a* STUDENT]

STUDENT

I only arrived a short while since
And humbly now make my appearance
To meet a man whose name I hear   1870
Spoken by one and all with awe.

MEPHISTO

I am delighted by your manners.
You see a man like many others.
You've looked at this and that already?

STUDENT

I beg you, take an interest in me.
I've come in very willing mood
With money enough and youthful blood.
Mother would hardly let me leave.
I want to learn something now I have.

MEPHISTO

This is the place for that, for certain.   1880

STUDENT

To be honest, I wish I was gone again.
These walls and halls are not at all
A world where I feel comfortable.
I'm cramped and cabined. I never see
Anything green and never a tree.
I sit in lecture rooms and feel
My hearing, sight and thinking fail.

MEPHISTO

It wants a little getting used to.
A babe won't take the mother's breast
Willingly from the word go   1890
But soon it suckles up with zest.
And at the breasts of wisdom likewise
Daily you'll feel your pleasure rise.

STUDENT

    I'll hang upon her neck in great delight.
    But how to get there? Will you put me right?

MEPHISTO

    Tell me, before continuing,
    What faculty will you be choosing?

STUDENT

    To become very learned is my ambition,
    I want to grasp all things in heaven
1900   And all upon the earth also.
    Knowledge I want and Mother Nature.

MEPHISTO

    You're on the right track there. Be sure
    You're not led off that strait and narrow.

STUDENT

    Body and soul I'm on it. Nonetheless,
    Of course, some freedom would not come amiss
    To pass the time in pleasant ways
    On sunny summer holidays.

MEPHISTO

    Use your time, it hurries off so fast.
    But Organization makes it last.
1910   You should accordingly attend
    Collegium Logicum first, my friend.
    There your mind will be put to rights
    And fitted tightly in Scotch boots
    So that in a more considered fashion
    It creeps the thought-road from then on
    And does not for example flit
    Like a will-o'-the-wisp this way and that.
    Day by day they'll teach you how
    The things you've done just so till now
1920   Heedlessly, like eating and drinking,
    You can't till logic's put to use.
    Though in the factory of thinking
    It's like a weaver's masterpiece:
    One kick and a thousand threads awake,
    The shuttles shoot to and fro,

The threads invisibly flow,
Thousandfold interlinking at a stroke –
Then enter the Philosopher
And proves these things must be as they are:
The first being thus, the second thus   1930
Therefore the third and fourth are thus
And were the first and second not there
Nor would the third and fourth be, ever.
And students marvel everywhere
At this, but none becomes a weaver.
To know a living thing and describe it
First they drive out the vital bit
And hold the parts but not the soul,
Alas, that made the parts a whole.
The Chemist calls it *encheiresis naturae*,   1940
Makes a fool of himself and can't see why.

STUDENT

I confess I don't fully follow you.

MEPHISTO

It will all be easier in a day or two
When you have learned the proper system
For reducing things and labelling them.

STUDENT

I'm mazed by it all as though I had
A mill-wheel going round in my head.

MEPHISTO

First after this it is the School
Of Metaphysics you must assail,
To plumb, by thinking, what the brain   1950
Of human beings can't contain;
And for what will and for what will not
Go in, get splendid words off pat.
But this half year your priority
Is to be as orderly as can be.
You have five hours a day. Do not
Fail to be there on the dot.
Go well prepared. Beforehand con
By rote the paragraphs one by one

1960   So you'll see clearer, when you look,
He's only said what's in the book.
But scribble with diligence as though
The Holy Ghost were dictating to you.

STUDENT

I shan't need telling twice. I'd say
The profit in it must be great:
You know where you are when you come away
With something down in black and white.

MEPHISTO

But choose a faculty, I beg you, do.

STUDENT

I think that Jurisprudence would not suit me.

MEPHISTO

1970   I think you not entirely blameworthy.
I do know what that discipline amounts to.
Laws and rights are handed on
Like an eternal malady.
They crawl from generation to generation
And shift from place to place, softly.
Good sense becomes nonsense, good deeds a cross.
Pity the grandchildren their lot.
But that right that is born with us
Alas, there's never any talk of that.

STUDENT

1980   You increase my aversion by what you say.
How happy those you teach must be!
Now I almost want to read Divinity.

MEPHISTO

I should not like to lead you astray.
It is so difficult in that science
To avoid wrong roads and hidden in it
There's so much poison and between it
And physicking there's not much difference.
Best in both you listen to only One
And let the Master's words be what you swear on.

1990   Stick – all in all – to words. Then through
The safest gate you'll pass into

The Temple of Certainty.

STUDENT

But there must be some meaning in the word.

MEPHISTO

No doubt. But don't torment yourself too hard.
For where a meaning's wanting there precisely
Up pops, on cue, a word.
With words first-class disputes are possible,
With words a system can be elevated,
Words are eminently believable,
Not one jot of a word can be abated.   2000

STUDENT

Forgive me, with all my questions I detain you
But I must trouble you further still.
Will you not say a vigorous word or two
On the subject of Medicine as well?
Three years soon goes
And far too wide the field, heaven knows.
But with a hint on where and how
We sooner feel our further way.

MEPHISTO [aside]

Enough of the dry tone. Must play
The devil again in earnest now.   2010
[Aloud] The spirit of Medicine is easy to apprehend.
You study the great world and the small
Through and through then let things wend
The way God wants it after all.
No use your roaming scientifically,
Each learns what he can and only that.
But the man who seizes the moment, he
Really knows what's what.
You have a good enough physique
And seem audacious too.   2020
Trust in yourself and that will make
Your fellow mortals trust in you.
Especially learn the way of leading women.
For all their myriad
And everlasting Jeremiad

In *one* place there's a sovereign medicine
And if you act halfways respectable
You'll bag them all.
Get letters after your name, then they'll believe
Few arts compare with yours.
You'll feel, the moment you arrive,
The bits that others slink around for years.
Acquire the knack of pressing nicely on the pulses,
With fire and slyness in your eyes
Grip her around her slim hips as you please
To find out how strait-laced she is.

STUDENT
That's a better prospect! There I see my way.

MEPHISTO
All theory, my friend, is grey.
Life's golden tree is green.

STUDENT
                                    Truly
I seem to dream. Will you allow me
To trouble you some other time and plumb,
By listening, your wisdom to the bottom?

MEPHISTO
What I can do I shall be glad to do.

STUDENT
How shall I ever take my leave of you?
Here is my album. I beg you, set
Some mark of your goodwill in it.

MEPHISTO
Very well.
    [*He writes, and hands back the album.*]

STUDENT [*reads*]
Eritis sicut Deus scientes bonum et malum.
    [*He closes the album reverently and takes his leave.*]

MEPHISTO
Follow the old words and my cousin, the Snake.
One day for sure in your godlikeness you'll quake.
    [*Enter* FAUST.]

FAUST

Where to?

MEPHISTO

Where your desires dictate.
We shall see the little world then the great.
What pleasure and what profit will be yours
In idling through the course!

FAUST

However, I am old and have
No easiness in the way I live.
This trial I make will not succeed,
The world and I have never agreed.
I feel so small under people's eyes,
I shall always be ill at ease.   2060

MEPHISTO

My dear friend, that will all come right.
You'll learn to live when you believe you might.

FAUST

How shall we quit this house? Have you
A coach, a coachman, horses somewhere?

MEPHISTO

We spread the cloak out, no more ado,
And it will ferry us through the air.
But see your baggage does not freight
Our enterprise with excess weight.
A little fiery air, prepared by me,
Up from the earth will lift us speedily   2070
And soonest if we're light. I offer
You my congratulations on your *vita nuova*!

Auerbach's Cellar in Leipzig

[*A party of drinkers.*]

FROSCH

Will nobody drink? Nobody laugh?
You look so glum. Shall I finish you off?

Like damp straw you are today
And usually you blaze away.

BRANDER

You're to blame. You do nothing,
Nothing stupid, nothing disgusting.

FROSCH [*pouring a glass of wine over his head*]
There's the two in one!

BRANDER

Twice the swine!

FROSCH

2080   You asked for it. The pleasure's mine.

SIEBEL

Quarrel outside if you want to quarrel.
Here sing up strong in turn now! Swill and bawl!
Tara boom! Tara boom!

ALTMAYER

Fetch cotton wool! The man
Will bust my eardrums with his din.

SIEBEL

When the rafters answer back we know
The bass is good and powerful here below.

FROSCH

And any man complaining throw him out!
Tra! Tra la la!

ALTMAYER

Tra! Tra la la!

FROSCH

And now we've tuned the throat.
[*He sings*]

2090   The Holy Roman Empire, bless its heart,
Why doesn't it fall apart?

BRANDER

A nasty song! Ugh! A political song,
A dismal song. Thank God daily
That the Holy Roman Empire's not your worry.
I at least think I'm better off for
Not being Emperor or Chancellor.

But we shan't go without a chief, I hope.
We shall elect ourselves a pope.
You know what sort of thing you must display
To be the man and tip the balance your way.   2100

FROSCH [*sings*]
    Sweet nightingale, rise up and bring
    Ten thousand greetings to my darling.

SIEBEL
    No greetings to a darling! I say no!

FROSCH
    Greetings and kisses also! I say so!
    [*He sings*]
    Lift the latch. The night is still.
    Lift the latch. My love's awake.
    The latch is down at daybreak.

SIEBEL
    Sing your song and sing her praises if you will.
    I'll have the laugh on you one of these days.
    She led me, and she'll lead you, by the nose.   2110
    I wish her a hobgoblin for a lover
    And she can neck with him where four ways meet
    And some old billy-goat off the Blocksberg give her,
    Galloping home, a goodnight bleat.
    An honest chap of real flesh and blood
    For trash like her's too good.
    Smashing her windows is about the only
    Greeting she will get from me.

BRANDER [*banging on the table*]
    Order! Order! Gentlemen,
    I do, admit it, know how to behave.   2120
    Sitting here are certain folk in love
    And I must honour their condition
    With a goodnight rendition.
    So hark! A song of the latest cut.
    And give the chorus all you've got!
    [*He sings*]
    There was a rat with a nest in the cellar,

He lived off fat and butter.
He grew himself a nice little belly
Like Doctor Martin Luther.
2130   The cook put poison out for him
And everything got tight for him
As though he had love in his guts.

CHORUS [*bawling joyfully*]
As though he had love in his guts!

BRANDER
He ran around and in and out
And supped from every puddle.
He gnawed and scratched the place about
But couldn't ease his trouble.
He jumped and jigged for fear of it,
Poor beast, he could take no more of it
2140   As though he had love in his guts.

CHORUS
As though he had love in his guts!

BRANDER
In terror he came in the light of day
And ran into the kitchen,
Fell on the hearth and gasped and lay
All pitiably twitching.
Whereat the poisoner in glee
'Ha! Ha! He's snuffing it,' says she,
'As though he had love in his guts.'

CHORUS
As though he had love in his guts!

SIEBEL
2150   Dolts, so the song amuses you?
You think she's clever putting out
Poison for the poor rats? Can't say I do.

BRANDER
They're special chums of yours no doubt.

ALTMAYER
Poor Fatty with the hairless pate!
He is made meek and mild by misery.

In a bloat rat he may contemplate
His image done by Nature to a tee.
   [*Enter* FAUST *and* MEPHISTOPHELES.]

MEPHISTO

Above all it must be my care
To bring you into cheerful company
So you will see how easy life can be.   2160
Every day's a holiday for the people here,
With little wit and much delight
They dance in a circle just as tight
As when a kitten chases its tail.
Except in the morning if their heads are thick
And as long as the landlord gives them tick
They are content and fear no ill.

BRANDER

These are travellers, lately come.
You can see it by the queer look of them.
I doubt they've been in the place an hour.   2170

FROSCH

Indeed. Leipzig, I'm proud of you! You are
A little Paris, a school of life.

SIEBEL

What do you take the strangers for?

FROSCH

Leave it to me. Fill one glass to the brim:
Easily as a milk tooth I'll draw,
Before it's empty, everything out of them.
Of the aristocracy, I'd say.
They have a proud and a displeased way.

BRANDER

Traders. I'll take a bet on that.

ALTMAYER

Perhaps.

FROSCH

      You watch, I'll put them through the mill.   2180

MEPHISTO [*to* FAUST]

These people never sniff the devil.

If he had them by the collar still they would not.

FAUST
Greetings to you, gentlemen.

SIEBEL
Thank you and likewise.
[*In an undertone, looking askance at* MEPHISTOPHELES]
Is the man a cripple? He limps as he goes.

MEPHISTO
Is it permitted to join you at your table?
Instead of good drink, there being none,
Your company will be enjoyable.

ALTMAYER
You seem a very spoilt man.

FROSCH
I daresay you left Rippach late
2190 And supped first with Hans Arse no doubt.

MEPHISTO
We did not call on him today
But had some talk with him the last time through.
On his relations he had much to say
And sends his greetings to the lot of you.
[*He bows to* FROSCH.]

ALTMAYER [*aside*]
You see! He knows what's what.

SIEBEL
Smart Alec, eh?

FROSCH
You wait. I'll have him. He'll not get away.

MEPHISTO
Was I mistaken or did we hear
Practised voices singing in a choir?
Song from this vaulting surely will
2200 Echo wonderfully well.

FROSCH
Are you perhaps a virtuoso?

MEPHISTO
No, no. I lack the strength, however great my gusto.

ALTMAYER
  Give us a song.
MEPHISTO
                    Dozens, at your command!
SIEBEL
  But let it be a brand new thing.
MEPHISTO
  We arrive from Spain, the sunny land
  And very home of drinking and of singing.
    [*He sings*]
    There was a king in history
    He had a giant flea . . .
FROSCH
  Hark at that! A flea! Not the best addition
  To present company in my opinion.   2210
MEPHISTO [*sings*]
    There was a king in history
    He had a giant flea.
    He loved him more than slightly
    Like his own progeny.
    The King sends for his tailor,
    His tailor he appears:
    Measure this Monseigneur
    And fit him with trousers.
BRANDER
  Only be sure to tell the tailor straight
  He'd better measure with the utmost care.   2220
  For if the trousers wrinkle anywhere
  The King will have his head on a plate.
MEPHISTO
    In silk he was and velvet
    Clothed from top to toe
    With ribbons on his doublet
    And a cross also.
    And at once they made him Minister
    He wore a big star.
    And soon his brothers and sisters
    Big at court they were.   2230

And all the lords and ladies
Were very sorely tried.
The Queen and all her maids they
Were bitten and eaten alive
And weren't allowed to crush them
Or scratch and make them go
But we can crush and squash them
Whenever we're bitten so.

CHORUS [*bawling joyfully*]
    But we can crush and squash them
2240   Whenever we're bitten so.

FROSCH
    Bravo! Bravo! The song was fine!

SIEBEL
    Let that be every flea's fate.

BRANDER
    With finger and thumb pince him tight!

ALTMAYER
    Here's to liberty! Here's to wine!

MEPHISTO
    I'd gladly raise a glass to liberty
    If your wines were somewhat better quality.

SIEBEL
    You've said that once too often already.

MEPHISTO
    I fear the landlord would protest.
    Otherwise I should treat
2250   This worthy company to our cellar's best.

SIEBEL
    Do so then. On my head be it!

FROSCH
    Produce a decent glass, we shall extol you.
    But give us more than tots to taste, will you?
    Justly to adjudicate on a sample
    I need a good gobful.

ALTMAYER [*in an undertone*]
    I have a feeling they are from the Rhine.

MEPHISTO
  Fetch me a borer.
BRANDER
                              What will you do with it?
  Are the casks outside? Have you brought your own?
ALTMAYER
  The landlord's tools are back there in a basket.
MEPHISTO [*taking the borer; to* FROSCH]
  What would you like to sample? Tell me.   2260
FROSCH
  How do you mean? Do you have a selection?
MEPHISTO
  I offer a choice to everyone.
ALTMAYER [*to* FROSCH]
   Already licking your lips, I see.
FROSCH
  Very well, if there's a choice, it's a Rhine wine I choose.
  Nothing's so good as what the fatherland bestows.
MEPHISTO [*boring a hole in the edge of the table where*
      FROSCH *is sitting*]
  We shall need stoppers. Fetch a little wax.
ALTMAYER
  Ach, this is the stuff of conjuring tricks.
MEPHISTO [*to* BRANDER]
   And you?
                  I want champagne
  And one that bubbles up with might and main.
    [MEPHISTOPHELES *bores a hole. In the meantime the wax*
    stoppers have been fashioned and are inserted.]
BRANDER
  We can't avoid what's foreign all the time.   2270
  Good things are often far from home.
  No honest German likes a Frenchman. All the same
  Their wines are very welcome.
SIEBEL [*as* MEPHISTOPHELES *comes to where he is sitting*]
  I must confess, sour things are not my choice.
  Give me a glass of the truly sweet.

MEPHISTO [*boring a hole*]
  At once. I think Tokay will suit.
ALTMAYER
  No, gentlemen, look me in the face.
  I see you are only making fun of us.
MEPHISTO
  Oh ho, in company as fine as this
2280 That would be daring a touch too far.
  Quickly now, no more ado,
  What wine may I offer you?
ALTMAYER
  Any. But no more palaver.
    [*Now all the holes have been made and stopped.*]
MEPHISTO [*with strange gestures*]
    Grapes on the stock of the vine,
    Horns on the billy-goat's head,
    Wine is a juice, the vinestock wood,
    And the wooden table brings forth wine!
    Look deep into Nature's secret.
    Here is a miracle, only believe it.

2290 Now draw the stoppers and drink your fill.
ALL [*as they draw the stoppers and the wines they asked for
      pour into their glasses*]
  Flowing for us, o bounteous well!
MEPHISTO
  Take care! Let none of it spill.
    [*They drink one glass after another.*]
ALL [*sing*]
    Oh we are as happy as cannibals
    Or half a thousand swine!
MEPHISTO
  The people are free. View their felicity.
FAUST
  I have a wish to leave here now.
MEPHISTO
  But first attend. Soon they will show
  Their brutishness in all its majesty.

SIEBEL [*drinks carelessly, the wine spills on the ground and
     becomes flame*]
   Help! Fire! Help! The flames of hell!
MEPHISTO [*commanding the flame*]
   Friendly element, be still.   2300
      [*To the company*]
   For now it was only a drop of purgatorial fire.
SIEBEL
   What is this? Wait! It will cost you dear.
   You seem not to know what kind of men we are.
FROSCH
   For the second time, will you give over?
ALTMAYER
   Best if he leaves the premises, I should say.
SIEBEL
   What, sir, you have the face
   To do your hocuspocus in this place?
MEPHISTO
   Quiet, you old sot.
SIEBEL
                        You witch's stick!
   Shall we have insults from you too?
BRANDER
   Oh now what blows will come your way!   2310
ALTMAYER [*draws a stopper out of the table, fire leaps up at
     him*]
   I'm burning, burning!
SIEBEL
                        Ho! Black magic!
   The man's an outlaw. Stick him through!
      [*They draw their knives and go for* MEPHISTOPHELES.]
MEPHISTO [*with an earnest gesture*]
   False word, false picture
   Change where and what you think you are.
   So, being here, be there!
      [*They stand in astonishment, looking at one another.*]
ALTMAYER
   Where am I? Such a lovely land!

FROSCH
  Vineyards! Do I see aright?
SIEBEL
                                         And grapes to hand!
BRANDER
  Here beneath this greenery
  See what a vine stock! What grapes! See!
    [*He seizes* SIEBEL *by the nose. Each seizes another's nose
    and all lift their knives.*]
MEPHISTO [*solemnly, as above*]
2320   Illusion, loose their eyesight's blindfold!
  Now take note how the devil plays.
    [*He disappears with* FAUST, *the drinkers leave go of one
    another.*]
SIEBEL
  What is happening?
ALTMAYER
                                         What?
FROSCH
                                         Was that your nose?
BRANDER [*to* Siebel]
  And it was your nose I held!
ALTMAYER
  It was a bolt, it passed through every limb.
  A chair! My knees are giving way!
FROSCH
  What has happened here? Will someone say?
SIEBEL
  Where is the man? If I lay hands on him
  He won't escape with his life, I swear.
ALTMAYER
  I saw him myself at the cellar door . . .
2330   On a barrel, riding away . . .
  I've lead weights weighing in my feet.
    [*Turning to the table*]
  Will wine, I wonder, still flow out?
SIEBEL
  All of it lies, deceit, moonshine!

FROSCH
  But it seemed to me I was drinking wine.
BRANDER
  And the bunches of grapes? What about those?
ALTMAYER
  And there are no miracles nowadays!

Witch's Kitchen

[*A low hearth, a large cauldron over the fire. Various
apparitions are visible in the rising steam. A meerkat sits
at the cauldron, skimming the froth off it and seeing that
it does not boil over. Her mate sits by her with their little
ones, warming himself. Walls and ceiling are hung with
the bizarre paraphernalia of a witch's household.*]
[*Enter* FAUST *and* MEPHISTOPHELES.]

FAUST
  I hate such bedlam witchery.
  You promise me I shall become
  A new man in this pandemonium?
  Shall I seek counsel from a crone?   2340
  And this dog's dinner cookery
  Will it slough thirty years off me?
  If you've no better stratagem
  I abandon hope, alas so soon.
  Has Nature never or some noble mind
  Devised a cure of any kind?
MEPHISTO
  Friend, now you are talking sense again. One may
  Also rejuvenate in a natural way
  But you will find that in another book
  And curious reading it would make.   2350
FAUST
  I wish to know it.
MEPHISTO
               The way without expense

And needing neither physician nor witch?
Betake yourself to the fields at once,
Begin to dig and delve and ditch.
Contain yourself, confine your mind
Within a very narrow sphere.
Nourish yourself on unmixed fare,
Live as a beast with beasts, think it not robbery
To dung the field you harvest with your dung.
2360   That is of all ways best, believe you me,
To live four score years young.

FAUST

I'm not accustomed. I could not abide
To learn the knack of handling a spade.
A narrow life will not suit me.

MEPHISTO

Therefore the witch is necessary.

FAUST

But why? Why have the old woman brew
The potion? Why can't you?

MEPHISTO

A fine pastime! While it bubbled away
I could build a thousand bridges, I daresay.
2370   Not only art, not only science
Are needful for it, also patience.
Quiet spirits work for years, only long length
Of time will give a subtle fermentation strength.
And what ingredients you need!
Very peculiar things indeed!
True, the devil taught her how.
The devil cannot do it though.
        [*Noticing the animals*]
See what a pretty little clan!
Here's the maid and there's the man.
        [*To the animals*]
2380   The mistress not at home, I suppose?

ANIMALS

        Gone carousing,

    Left the house,
    Up the chimney, off she goes!
MEPHISTO
    How long does she go gadding for?
ANIMALS
    The time we warm our paws. No more.
MEPHISTO [*to* FAUST]
    How do you find the wee beasties?
FAUST
    Of all I've seen, among the foulest.
MEPHISTO
    No, conversation such as this
    Is just the sort I like the best.
    [*To the animals*]
    Tell me, my maledicted loves,   2390
    What sort of broth are you stirring there?
ANIMALS
    Broth for the undeserving poor.
MEPHISTO
    Oh, they'll be along to sup in droves.
MALE MEERKAT [*approaches and fawns on* MEPHISTO-
    PHELES]
    Throw the dice quick
    And make me rich.
    Roll them my way,
    Everything's awry,
    If I had the loot
    I could think straight.
MEPHISTO
    What a cheerful monkey he would be   2400
    If he could play the lottery!
    [*Meanwhile the little meerkats have been playing with a
    large sphere and now roll it forward.*]
MALE MEERKAT
    So the world spins,
    It rises and falls
    And forever rolls.

Like glass it rings,
Then it's smithereens!
It's hollow within.
How it glitters here!
And here even more!
2410   By my living soul!
Dear boy of mine
You keep away!
You will surely die,
It is made of clay,
Shards will fly!

MEPHISTO
  Why the sieve?
MALE MEERKAT [*fetching it down*]
  If you should thieve
  I'd know it right away.
  [*He runs over to his mate and lets her look through the
  sieve.*]
  Look through the sieve,
2420   You know the thief
  And don't dare say?
MEPHISTO [*going to the fire*]
  And what's this pot?
MALE AND FEMALE MEERKATS
  Dumbclot!
  He doesn't know the pot,
  He doesn't know the cauldron!
MEPHISTO
  Ill-mannered crittur!
MALE MEERKAT
  Take the fly swatter!
  Here's a chair to sit on.
  [*He obliges* MEPHISTOPHELES *to sit down.*]
FAUST [*who all this time has been standing in front of a
  mirror, now moving closer, now moving away from it*]
  What am I seeing? What am I being shown?
2430   O heavenly image in the magic glass!
  Oh give me wings, love, let me cross

With you, swiftly as may be into her domain.
Oh if I do not keep my place
But nerve myself and move in close
I seem to lose her in a mist –
Loveliest image of any woman!
Is it possible? Such beauty there is in women?
See how she lies! Of every kind of heaven
There in her body the essence is manifest.
And things like this are to be found on earth?   2440

MEPHISTO
Naturally, when a god has slogged six days
And gives himself on the seventh a word of praise
You would expect the result to have some worth.
For now, until your eyes are full, behold!
I can sniff you out a sweetheart such as this.
Happy the man whose lot it is
To carry one like her over his threshold.
      [*While* FAUST *still gazes into the mirror,* MEPHISTO-
      PHELES, *stretching himself in the chair and playing with
      the fly swatter, continues*]
I sit here like the king upon his throne.
I have the sceptre, all I want's the crown.

THE ANIMALS [*who in the meantime have been up to all
      manner of strange and unconnected tricks, now, screech-
      ing loudly, bring* MEPHISTOPHELES *a crown*]
      Oh be so good   2450
      And glue the crown
      With your sweat and blood.
      [*They handle the crown carelessly and break it in two
      halves, with which they then leap around.*]
      Oh calamity!
      We hear, speak and see,
      We rhyme every line –

FAUST [*to the mirror*]
   Alas for me, I shall go stark mad.

MEPHISTO [*pointing to the animals*]
   Now even my head's near to reeling.

ANIMALS
>   And if we can do it
>   And if it will fit
2460 >   What *thoughts* we'll have had!
FAUST [*to the mirror*]
>   The heart in me begins to feel like fire.
>   Quickly now, let us leave here.
MEPHISTO [*gesturing as above*]
>   Well at least we must admit
>   That they are poets, the real thing.
>> [*The cauldron, neglected by the female meerkat, begins to boil over. A large flame is produced and escapes up the chimney. Down through the flame, with frightful shrieks, comes the* WITCH.]
WITCH
>   Ow! Ow! Ow! Ow!
>   Cursed creature! Damned she-swine!
>   Raise a flame and scorch the Dame!
>   Cursed creature!
>> [*She notices* FAUST *and* MEPHISTOPHELES.]
>   What is this here?
2470 >   Who is this here?
>   What do you want?
>   Who has crept in?
>   Fire pains
>   In all your bones!
>> [*She thrusts the stirring spoon into the cauldron and splashes flames at* FAUST, MEPHISTOPHELES *and the animals. The animals whimper.*]
MEPHISTO [*reversing the swatter in his hand, strikes with the stick among the jars and pots*]
>   Break! Broke!
>   There's your mess
>   And there's the glass!
>   Only a joke,
>   The beat, foul thing,
2480 >   To what you sing.
>> [*The* WITCH *retreats in fury and horror.*]

Finally, eyesore! Finally, carrion
You know your lord and master, do you?
Suppose I strike, as I've a mind to,
And smash you and your cat-coven?
My red coat wakes no reverence?
You do not recognize the cockerel plume?
Have I obscured my countenance?
Shall I perhaps name my own name?

WITCH

Oh sir, forgive this rough welcome.
I see no cloven hoof and no   2490
Two ravens. What has become of them?

MEPHISTO

On this occasion that will do
For punishment. And, to be fair,
It is a while since we two met.
And with the advance of Culture everywhere
Even the devil needs a lick of it.
The nordic phantom fades away,
Horns and tail and claws have had their day.
And as to the foot, beyond my power to lose,
It would only set me down in people's eyes.   2500
And so, like many a young gentleman,
For years I've let cosmetics help me where they can.

WITCH [capering]

My head's away, my wits are gone!
Sir Satan visits me again!

MEPHISTO

Woman, I will not hear that name!

WITCH

Why not? What has it done to you?

MEPHISTO

It went the way of legend long ago.
The human lot however stayed the same.
Rid of the Evil One. And the evildoers? Oh no.
Call me Baron, that will be best.   2510
I am a gentleman like other gentlemen,
My blue blood is beyond suspicion,

And here's my family crest.
 [*He makes an indecent gesture.*]
WITCH [*laughing uproariously*]
 Ha! Ha! Ha! Ha! That's how you are!
 A rogue! A rogue, as you always were!
MEPHISTO [*to* FAUST]
 Mark, my friend, and understand. This is
 The right way to behave with witches.
WITCH
 Now gentlemen, what brings you to this place?
MEPHISTO
 We want a good glass of the famous juice,
2520 And of the oldest, if you please.
 The virtue of it doubles with the years.
WITCH
 I have a bottle here. It's one
 I take a nip myself of on occasion
 And that no longer, not the least bit, stinks.
 I'll pour you a tot of it with pleasure.
 [*Aside to* MEPHISTOPHELES]
 But if this man is unprepared, and drinks
 You know he will not live an hour more.
MEPHISTO
 He is my friend and it will do him good.
 Give him your kitchen's best, I shall be glad.
2530 So draw your circle, speak the spell
 And fill him up a beakerful.
 [*The* WITCH, *gesticulating strangely, draws a circle and*
 places various wondrous objects within it. Meanwhile the
 glasses begin to ring and the cauldrons to resound in a sort
 of music. Finally she fetches a large book and places the
 meerkats in the circle to serve her as a lectern and to hold
 the torch. She beckons FAUST.]
FAUST [*to* MEPHISTOPHELES]
 What good, tell me, is in these things?
 Mad rigmarole and crazy handwavings,
 The foulest kind of trickery,
 All known and all detestable to me.

MEPHISTO
  All nonsense, all ridiculous.
  Don't be so harsh on her and it.
  She must, like any doctor, do her hocuspocus
  So that the juice will bring you benefit.
    [*He obliges* FAUST *to enter the circle.*]
WITCH [*in a very rhetorical manner begins reading aloud
      from the book*]
  Hear how it's done!   2540
  Make ten from one
  And let two be
  And also three
  And then you're rich!
  Forfeit the four!
  From five and six,
  So says the witch,
  Make seven and eight.
  The end's in sight!
  And nine is one   2550
  And ten is none.
  The witch's times-table is done!
FAUST
  The old woman's in delirium.
MEPHISTO
  Still there's a good deal more to come.
  I know full well. The whole book sounds the same.
  I did myself once let it waste my time.
  For total nonsense mystifies
  Alike the foolish and the wise.
  My friend, the trick is old and new.
  It always was the way, to put   2560
  By Three and One and One and Three
  Error and not the truth about.
  And so they teach and blather what they please.
  To take such fools to task is too much trouble,
  And people hearing words mostly suppose
  There must be thinking going on as well.

WITCH [*continuing*]
>   The high puissance
>   Of knowledge and science
>   From the whole world hidden
2570 >   Is given unbidden
>   To him who never
>   Thinks or makes any endeavour.

FAUST
>   What nonsense is it she's reciting?
>   My head cannot withstand much more.
>   I seem to hear an entire choir
>   Of a hundred thousand madmen spouting.

MEPHISTO
>   Enough, enough, my brave sibyl!
>   Offer your drink and fill
>   The bowl at once now to the brim.
2580 >   My friend here ranks high in the hierarchy
>   And has downed much good drink already.
>   Your potion will not harm him.
>   [*The* WITCH *with extreme ceremoniousness pours the*
>   *potion into a dish. When* FAUST *raises it to his lips there*
>   *is a flicker of flame.*]

MEPHISTO
>   Be resolute. Come, drink it down.
>   Your heart will feel the joy of it very soon.
>   Best friends with the devil, you won't allow
>   A little flame to halt you now?
>   [*The* WITCH *undoes the circle.* FAUST *steps out.*]
>   Quickly, come out. You must not stand still.

WITCH
>   I wish you joy of your little tipple.

MEPHISTO [*to the* WITCH]
>   If I can oblige you in any way
2590 >   On Walpurgis Night you have only to say.

WITCH
>   Here is a song. If you sing it now and then
>   You'll feel it work most particularly.

MEPHISTO [*to* FAUST]
  Make haste now. Come, be led by me.
  It is imperative you sweat to hurry
  The virtue through the inner and the outer man.
  Later I'll teach you to prize a noble idleness
  And soon you'll feel with keen gladness
  Cupid stir and leap and leap again.

FAUST
  One look more in the mirror quickly, please.
  The image of the woman was so beautiful.   2600

MEPHISTO
  No, no. In flesh the paragon of all
  Women will stand soon before your very eyes.
     [*Aside*]
  That drink in you, you will see Helen
  Soon enough in every woman.

Street

     [FAUST, MARGARETE *passing by.*]
FAUST
  May I offer my arm and accompany
  A beautiful lady on her way?

MARGARETE
  Am neither a lady nor beautiful,
  Can make my own way home very well.
                          [*She frees herself and exits.*]

FAUST
  Heavens, the child is beautiful!
  I never saw anything comparable.   2610
  So proper and so virtuous
  And yet with a touch of sauciness.
  Her cheeks so bright, her lips so red,
  I'll not forget it till I am dead.
  The way she cast her eyes down

Deep it has marked this heart of mine.
And then how sharp she was with me!
Ravishing as anything can be!
  [*Enter* MEPHISTOPHELES.]

FAUST

Listen, get me that girl. You must.

MEPHISTO

What girl?

FAUST

2620   The one who just went past.

MEPHISTO

Her? She's come from seeing the priest.
He has absolved her of all her sins.
I crept by the box, I was listening.
She's a very innocent young thing
And nothing at all in her confessions.
I have no power over her.

FAUST

She's older than fourteen however.

MEPHISTO

The way you talk! Like Dirty Dick –
Wants every lovely bloom, and quick,
2630 And every honour, so he supposes,
And favour's for plucking when he chooses.
But that's not always how it goes.

FAUST

Spare me the law and the homily,
Mr Know-All, will you, please?
I tell you here and I tell you straight
If that sweet thing this very night
Doesn't lie in my arms, then you and I
At midnight go our separate ways.

MEPHISTO

Think what can and can't be done.
2640 Even to sniff out an occasion
Fourteen days is the least I'll need.

FAUST

If I had even seven hours spare

I would not need the devil's aid
To seduce a little thing like her.

MEPHISTO

You talk like a Frenchman already – well, nearly.
But don't, I beg you now, be surly.
What use is it to enjoy toot sweet?
The pleasure is nowhere near so great
As when you first by toing and froing
And fuss and bother and much adoing   2650
Soften the dolly right. Which is
What many an Italian story teaches.

FAUST

I've an appetite without all that.

MEPHISTO

Joking and complaints aside,
Be told by me, like it or not,
With that beautiful child: more haste, less speed.
Storming won't take her. We must bend
Ourselves to cunning to achieve our end.

FAUST

Get me something of the angel's own,
Conduct me where the girl lies down,   2660
Get me a scarf from her sweet breast,
A garter of hers for my love and lust.

MEPHISTO

So you may see my willingness
To further and serve you in your distress
Not a moment will we waste: I'll bring
You into her room by evening.

FAUST

And shall I see her? And have her?

MEPHISTO

                         No.

She will be visiting a neighbour.
But all alone in the meantime you
On all the hope of future pleasure   2670
Can sate yourself in her atmosphere.

FAUST
  Can we go now?
MEPHISTO
                          Too early yet.
FAUST
  She needs a present. See to it.

                                                    [*Exit.*]

MEPHISTO
  Presents already? Bravo! She'll give him something back.
  There's many a lovely place I know
  And many a treasure buried long ago.
  I must see what I have in stock.

                                                    [*Exit.*]

Evening

  [*A clean and tidy little room.* MARGARETE *plaiting and
  putting up her hair.*]

MARGARETE
  I'd give a lot to find out who
  That gentleman could have been today.
2680 A proper sort of man, I'd say
  And of a noble family too,
  I could tell from his look – also that he
  Was forward in his way with me.

                                                    [*Exit.*]

  [*Enter* FAUST *and* MEPHISTOPHELES.]
MEPHISTO
  In now, but very quietly. Come.
FAUST [*after a silence*]
  I beg you, let me be alone.
MEPHISTO [*sniffing around*]
  Not all girls keep the place so clean.

                                                    [*Exit.*]

FAUST [*looking up and around*]
  Sweet evening radiance in this sanctum,

Weaving the air of it, welcome!
Fasten on my heart, sweet pains of love,
That on the dew of hope thirstily live.   2690
Breath and the feel of stillness round me,
Of order and contentedness,
What abundance in this poverty
And in this prison such a blessedness!
    [*He throws himself into a leather armchair by the bed.*]
Accept me now, having been so long
The embracer of past worlds of joy and care.
How often to this fatherly throne have clung
The children clambering in a throng.
Perhaps my darling here at Christmastide
With chubby cheeks in childish gratitude   2700
Has kissed the sere hand of an ancestor.
Girl, how I feel your spirit like the breath
Of order and abundance here
Daily directing you as would a mother
To spread the table with a clean cloth
And strew the rippling sand over the floor.
Beloved hand, giving as the gods have given,
Of this poor place you make a kingdom of heaven.
And here!
    [*He raises a curtain of the bed*]
            Grips me in terror and delight!
Here let me bide full hours of my time.   2710
Here Nature, in a gentle dream,
Shaped a born angel to her perfect state.
Here the child lay, her young breast swelled
With warm life and here
The weaving gods revealed
Their holy image pure in her.

And you? What purpose have you here?
The place has touched me to the core.
What is it you want? Why does the heart sink so?
Faustus, wretch, I do not know you.   2720

Like scent, is there a magic round me here?
I wanted my enjoyment of her fast
And melt now in a dream of love. So must
We bend to every pressure of the air?

And were she now, this minute, to appear
How you would pay for the wrong you have done to her!
So swaggering big you were, so small
Before her feet in tears you'd crawl.

MEPHISTO [*entering*]
Be quick, I see her coming below.

FAUST

2730   Let us go! I'll never come back. Let us go!

MEPHISTO
Here is a casket, and heavy too.
I fetched it hither from elsewhere.
Put it in the cupboard all the same.
It will make her giddy, I promise you.
I stowed a few little things in there
To win you another. But it's all one:
A child's a child whatever the game.

FAUST
I don't know. Should I?

MEPHISTO
                              Why the question?
Have you a mind to keep the treasure?

2740   Then I advise Your Lechery
To waste your time in some other fashion
And spare me any further bother.
I hope you are not miserly?
I scratch my head, I employ my hands –
    [*he places the casket in the cupboard and locks the door
    again*]
Away now quickly! –
To bend the sweet young thing the way
Your heart desires and commands
And you look as though
The lecture hall awaited you

And Physics and Metaphysics stood   2750
Greyly before you in flesh and blood.
Away!

                      [*Exit* FAUST *and* MEPHISTOPHELES.]

MARGARETE [*entering with a lamp*]
  It is so close and heavy in here.
    [*She opens the window.*]
  And yet not very warm out there.
  I feel . . . I don't know what I feel –
  I wish my mother were home again.
  My flesh creeps, my blood runs chill –
  Ach, I'm a foolish timid woman.
    [*She begins to sing while she undresses.*]
    There was a king in Thule
    True till time shall stop.
    His sweetheart, dying, gave him   2760
    A golden drinking cup.

    No thing to him was dearer
    And never did he raise
    Nor ever did he empty it
    But tears filled his eyes.

    And when he came to dying
    And all his goods were told
    His son and heir had everything
    Except the cup of gold.   2770

    The King sat at his banquet
    And all his knights were there
    In the high hall of his fathers
    In the castle on the shore.

    He drank the dying glimmer
    Of life with love and threw
    The holy golden drinking cup
    Into the waves below

And watched it falling, drinking
2780   And sinking in the sea
And saw no more and drank no more
This side eternity.
[*She opens the cupboard to put away her clothes and sees
the jewel box.*]
How did the pretty casket get in here?
I locked the cupboard up, I'm sure.
How strange! What might be in the box, I wonder.
Did someone bring it as security
And Mother lent them money on it?
There on the ribbon's a little key.
I've a good mind to open it.
2790   What's this? Dear God in heaven! Look there!
I never saw such a thing before.
Jewels! A lady dressed in these
Could appear on high days and holy days.
How would the necklace look on me?
I wonder whose these fine things are.
[*She puts on some of the jewellery and steps before the
mirror.*]
If only the earrings belonged to me.
I look quite different straight away.
What use is beauty and young blood?
Of course, all that is fine and good
2800   But that is all it ever is,
There's always pity in their praises.
What everyone wants
And all that counts
Is gold. Poor things, alas for us.

Promenade

[FAUST *walking pensively to and fro. Enter* MEPHISTO-
PHELES.]

MEPHISTO

By the spurning of love! By the fires of hell!
I wish I knew a worse thing to swear by that as well.

FAUST

What's wrong? What's eating you alive?
I never saw such a face. What is it?

MEPHISTO

If I wasn't a devil myself I'd give
Me up to the Devil this very minute.   2810

FAUST

Has something in your head come away?
Raving becomes you, I must say.

MEPHISTO

That jewellery – who'd have believed it? –
Got for Gretchen, a priest has thieved it!
It came under the mother's eyes,
Gave her the secret heebie-jeebies.
The woman has a very fine nose,
Snuffles in the prayer-book wherever she goes.
She sniffs your goods and can always tell
Profane from sacred by the smell   2820
And she sensed the jewels didn't bring
Much with them in the way of a blessing.
Child, she cried, ill-gotten gains
Devour the blood, put the soul in chains.
We'll offer them up to the Mother of God,
She'll treat us to manna from heaven instead.
Poor little Margaret's mouth went down,
She thinks it's a gift horse when all's said and done
And verily, it wasn't a godless man
Who fetched it hither in that sweet fashion.   2830
But Mother sent for a priest and he

Soon as he heard the whole story
He liked the look of the things he saw
And said: 'Such is the proper spirit.
Who overcometh shall inherit.
The Church has an admirable maw,
Has gobbled up whole lands and yet
Was never ever surfeited.
Only the Church, dear ladies, can
2840   Digest gains that are ill-gotten.'

FAUST
It is a very common game.
Jews and kings do the same.

MEPHISTO
And scoops up bangles, necklets, rings
As though they were ten-a-penny things
And no more thank-you-very-much
Than you'd give for a bag of nuts or such.
Promised them both rewards in heaven
To their great gratification.

FAUST
And Gretchen?

MEPHISTO
                                    Restless. She doesn't know
2850   What it is she wants or should want now.
Day and night she thinks of the gold and silver
But more of him who brought it her.

FAUST
My darling's trouble grieves me.
Get her more jewels immediately.
The first were nothing special, were they?

MEPHISTO
To His Lordship everything is child's play.

FAUST
Do it. Sort things so they suit me.
Attach yourself to her neighbour. Be
Less like cold porridge. Move. Rustle
2860   Her up a new adornment, devil.

MEPHISTO
    Gladly, Your Lordship. Yes, of course.

                          [*Exit* FAUST.]

    A fool in love like that will blow
    The sun and moon and all the stars
    To amuse his sweetheart an hour or so.

                                [*Exit.*]

At the Neighbour's House

    [MARTHE *alone.*]

MARTHE
    God forgive my husband, he
    Has not done the right thing by me.
    Into the wide world he has flown
    And left me in the bed alone
    For all I never gave him grief.
    God knows, I was a loving wife. [*She weeps.*]   2870
    Perhaps he's dead! – Oh the pain of it! –
    If only I had a certificate.
       [*Enter* MARGARETE.]

MARGARETE
    Frau Marthe!

MARTHE
             What is it, Gretelchen?

MARGARETE
    My knees are giving under me!
    I've found a box in my cupboard again
    Like the other one but of ebony
    And things in it, so lovely, and far
    More precious than the ones before.

MARTHE
    Don't tell your mother or like the last
    She'll hie them away to confession fast.   2880

MARGARETE
    Oh but look at them! Oh see here!

MARTHE [*dressing her in the jewellery*]
  What a lucky creature you are, to be sure.

MARGARETE
  But I can't be seen on the street like this
  Nor ever in church in them, alas.

MARTHE
  Whenever you like come over to me
  And put them on in secrecy,
  Walk up and down in the mirror an hour
  And that will give us pleasure.
  And then there'll be some grand occasion
2890 When you can show them people bit by bit,
  A little necklace first, then the pearl earrings on.
  Mother won't notice. Or you fib about it.

MARGARETE
  Who brought the boxes? Who could it be?
  Something's at work that should not be.
      [*A knock at the door.*]
  Is that my mother? Oh God in heaven!

MARTHE [*peeping through the curtain*]
  A stranger. A gentleman. – Come in!
      [*Enter* MEPHISTOPHELES.]

MEPHISTO
  I enter without more ado
  And beg your pardon for doing so.
      [*At the sight of* MARGARETE *he steps back with a great
      show of respect.*]
  Frau Marthe Schwerdtlein I was looking for.

MARTHE
2900 That's me, sir. What do you have to say?

MEPHISTO [*aside to her*]
  I know you now. I need not stay.
  You have an important visitor.
  Forgive me, do. I importune.
  I'll call again in the afternoon.

MARTHE [*aloud*]
  Well fancy that, child. Goodness me!
  The gentleman takes you for a fine lady.

MARGARETE

  I'm a poor young girl. The gentleman shows
  Me too much kindness, heaven knows.
  The pearls and the necklace are not mine.

MEPHISTO

  Oh it's not the jewellery alone   2910
  But your bright eyes and the way you have.
  How glad I am that I need not leave.

MARTHE

  What brings you then? I long to know . . .

MEPHISTO

  Would I had better news. I fear
  Your punishing the messenger.
  Your husband's dead and says hello.

MARTHE

  Dead? Oh alas! Oh my faithful love!
  My husband's dead! I cannot live!

MARGARETE

  Oh dear Frau Marthe, don't despair!

MEPHISTO

  Let me recount the sad affair.   2920

MARGARETE

  All life long better not to love
  If loss should sadden me to the grave.

MEPHISTO

  Mirth to sorrow, sorrow to mirth.

MARTHE

  Recount the end of his life on earth.

MEPHISTO

  His grave is with Saint Antony
  In Padua. He beds in peace
  In that well-consecrated place
  Cool for all eternity.

MARTHE

  And you bring nothing else to me?

MEPHISTO

  I do. This large and onerous request: 2930
  That with three hundred masses you sing his soul to rest.

I've nothing else from him in my pocket.

MARTHE

What! No medallion? Bangle? Necklet?
When every journeyman deep in his pack
Has some such keepsake he will go
Hungry or beg sooner than hock.

MEPHISTO

Madam, I'm very sorry. Yet
In truth he spent his money well. Also
He greatly rued the error of his ways.
2940   Much more, however, his miseries.

MARGARETE

Alas, how unhappy is the human lot!
I'll pray and pray for him, indeed I will.

MEPHISTO

You ought to marry at once. Why not?
Being, as you are, so young and lovable.

MARGARETE

Oh no, not yet. It wouldn't be right.

MEPHISTO

If not a husband, a lover while you wait.
What greater gift of heaven than
The sweet embrace of man and woman?

MARGARETE

That is not the custom here.

MEPHISTO

2950   Custom or not, it does occur.

MARTHE

What else? Tell.

MEPHISTO

                    I stood by the bed he died in,
It was better than a midden at any rate,
Of straw, half-rotten. He died as a Christian
And found there were many things left on the slate.
'How I loathe myself,' he cried, 'from top to toe!
To leave my trade and my poor wife so!
The thought will kill me. Oh if only,
Before it does, she had forgiven me!'

MARTHE [*weeping*]
  Dear, good man, I forgave him long ago.
MEPHISTO
  'Although, God knows, she was more to blame than me.'   2960
MARTHE
  Lies! With his dying breath too. Oh the liar!
MEPHISTO
  He was raving at the last for sure.
  (In such things I have some experience.)
  'No time to stand and stare,' he said.
  'I gave her children, I gave her bread –
  Bread in the widest possible sense –
  And could not even eat my share in peace.'
MARTHE
  So faithlessly from memory to efface
  The wife who shifted for him night and day!
MEPHISTO
  No, no. He turned his loving thoughts your way.   2970
  He said: 'From Malta putting out to sea
  I prayed with fervour for my wife and family
  And heaven was kind and let us seize
  A Turkish vessel as a prize
  Carrying treasure for the Gran Signior.
  Then bravery had its recompense
  And I received my proper quittance
  Paid to me in full measure.'
MARTHE
  But what? And where? Perhaps he buried it?
MEPHISTO
  Who knows where the four winds carried it?   2980
  A lady took an interest in his welfare
  In Naples strolling as a stranger there.
  She showed him such love and devotion
  He felt it till the last unction.
MARTHE
  To his own children – oh the rogue and thief!
  Not all his misery, all his need
  Was any hindrance on his wicked life.

MEPHISTO

Indeed. And, serve him right, he died.
Madam, if I were in your shoes
2990   I'd mourn him one year and be virtuous
And spy to take a new love when I chose.

MARTHE

Alas, one like my first one was
Will hardly come my way again.
For love and laughter he had no equal
But loved the wandering life too well
And other women and other wine
And that damned gaming pastime.

MEPHISTO

Well, well, there might be no objection
If he, for his part, much the same
3000   Turned a blind eye in your direction.
On terms like that, I swear to you,
You and I might swap rings too.

MARTHE

The gentleman will have his joke.

MEPHISTO [*aside*]

I must not leave it long till I depart.
She'd not let even the devil off the hook.

   [*To* GRETCHEN]

And how are you in matters of the heart?

MARGARETE

What does the gentleman mean?

MEPHISTO [*aside*]

                You innocent child.

   [*Aloud*]

Goodbye, ladies.

MARGARETE

        Goodbye.

MARTHE

           Sir, quickly may I be told

How I might come by a certificate,
3010   My darling's death and burial, the how, when, where of it?
I always did want all things right and proper.

I want to read him dead in the newspaper.
MEPHISTO

For a thing to be true it needs two witnesses,
Dear lady, who will say it is.
I have an excellent friend, he'll stand
In court for you and raise his hand.
I'll bring him here.

MARTHE

                    Oh indeed do.

MEPHISTO

And the young lady will be present too?
He's a gentleman, has travelled widely
And shows the ladies every courtesy.   3020

MARGARETE

With such a man I'd blush for shame.

MEPHISTO

No need, and were it the King who came.

MARTHE

Behind my house, there in my garden,
This evening we await the gentlemen.

Street

[FAUST *and* MEPHISTOPHELES.]
FAUST

Well? Are we moving? Are we nearly there?

MEPHISTO

Bravo! I find you all on fire.
In no time now Gretchen is yours.
You'll see her this evening at her neighbour's
Marthe, a woman as if made
For coupling and gypsy trade.   3030

FAUST

Good.

MEPHISTO

          But something is asked of us as well.

FAUST

A quid pro quo is usual.

MEPHISTO

Nothing but that we solemnly attest
Her husband, dead and done with, is at rest
In Padua, in a consecrated place.

FAUST

How clever! And first we go and see?

MEPHISTO

Sancta simplicitas! That won't be necessary.
Swearing without knowing will suffice.

FAUST

If that's your best idea the plan falls through.

MEPHISTO

3040   Hark at the man! Such saintliness!
And never in all your days have you
Once borne false witness?
Nor ever did with might and main
Hold forth in brazen shamelessness
On God, the World and all that moves therein
And Man and all that stirs in his heart and head?
And yet the truth is on that score,
Confess, you never did know more
Than you do about Herr Schwerdtlein's being dead.

FAUST

3050   You are, and always will be, a liar, a sophist.

MEPHISTO

Well, if one did not always know the rest . . .
For tomorrow, honourable as you are,
Will you not turn poor Gretchen's head and swear
Your soul's entire love for her?

FAUST

And mean it too.

MEPHISTO

                No doubt you will.
And then true love for evermore,
The one desire that's sovereign everywhere . . .
And will you mean all that as well?

FAUST

Leave off! I will! – When I feel
And for the feeling, for the turmoil,   3060
Look for names and looking fail
And trawl the world with all my senses
And snatch after the highest words of all
And say the fire that burns me is
Without an end in space or time –
Is that a devilish lying game?

MEPHISTO

Still I am right.

FAUST

Hear this. Take note –
And be so kind and save me saying it twice –
It's easy being in the right
If all you hear is your own voice.   3070
Come now. I'm sick of talk. For you
Are right. Chief reason is: I have to.

Garden

[MARGARETE *on* FAUST'*s arm,* MARTHE *and* MEPHISTO-
PHELES *walking up and down.*]

MARGARETE

I'm sure the gentleman is only being kind,
Shames me, comes down to my level.
A traveller will often find
The best in things, to be agreeable.
In my poor talk, I'm well aware,
There's little for a man as travelled as you are.

FAUST

One look from you, one word outbids the sum
Of all this world's wisdom. [*He kisses her hand.*]   3080

MARGARETE

Don't bring yourself to that! How can you?
I have such rough and ugly hands,

Every kind of work they have always had to do.
My mother makes such strict demands.
   [*They pass across.*]

MARTHE

And you, sir, always under way?

MEPHISTO

Alas that work and duty drive us!
Though the leaving of many a place may grieve us,
Whatever we wish, we cannot stay.

MARTHE

All very well in the nimble years maybe
3090   To wander the world footloose and fancy free.
But an ill time comes on
And dragging his sole self to the grave no wifeless man
Has ever thought much fun.

MEPHISTO

I view the distant prospect with horror.

MARTHE

Sir, be advised betimes therefore.
   [*They pass across.*]

MARGARETE

Out of sight out of mind is true.
Polite ways come easily to you
But you have friends and many of them
And they are cleverer than I am.

FAUST

3100   Dear girl, believe me, what they call clever
Is often more dumb conceit.

MARGARETE

                 How can that be?

FAUST

Oh, that innocence and simplicity
Don't know themselves and their own sacred value ever!
That the meek, the lowly, whom the greatest
Of loving Nature's gifts are given to –

MARGARETE

Think of me for a little while at least.
I shall have time enough to think of you.

FAUST
  No doubt you are much alone?
MARGARETE
  Yes, our household is a small one
  But still the work has to be done.   3110
  We don't have a maid. I have to cook, sweep, knit
  And sew and run around from morn till night.
  And everything, my mother wants it
  Always just right.
  Not that she really needs to straiten herself so.
  We might go about far more than many.
  My father left us a nice legacy,
  A little house outside the town and a garden too.
  But my days are very quiet now.
  My brother is a soldier.   3120
  My little sister died.
  True, with the child I was sorely tried.
  But I'd gladly have my trials again with her.
  I loved the child so.
FAUST
                      Angel, as you are, so was she.
MARGARETE
  I brought her up. And she dearly loved me.
  She was born after my father died.
  Mother we gave up for dead
  She lay so ill
  And she recovered very slowly, little by little.
  There was no question she could feed   3130
  The poor mite herself. Instead
  I raised her all on my own
  With milk and water. It made her mine.
  In my arms, in my lap, she
  Wriggled, grew, was sweet to me.
FAUST
  Surely the purest happiness was yours.
MARGARETE
  But surely also many heavy hours.
  The baby's cradle stood at night

By my bed. She only had to stir
3140 I was awake and might
Have to take her in with me or feed her
Or when she wouldn't stop crying go
Dancing the bedroom with her to and fro
And be at the washtub in the morning early
Then at the market and the stove, busy
On and on and like today tomorrow.
In all that, sir, you are not always at your best
But sweeter for it are your food and rest.
    [*They pass across.*]

MARTHE
Pity us women. How shall we persuade
3150 A man who is not the marrying kind?

MEPHISTO
A woman of your sort might be what I need
To prove me wrong and make me change my mind.

MARTHE
Have you found nothing yet? Say yes or no.
The heart still unattached wherever you go?

MEPHISTO
No place like home, so the saying is.
And a virtuous wife's worth more than rubies.

MARTHE
I mean, have you never felt the desire?

MEPHISTO
I've had a courteous welcome everywhere.

MARTHE
I meant, was your heart never in earnest?

MEPHISTO
3160 With women it is never right to jest.

MARTHE
Oh, you don't understand!

MEPHISTO
                    Do I not? Oh dear.
But I do understand – how very kind you are.
    [*They pass across.*]

FAUST

   You little angel, you knew me again
   There in the garden the moment I came in?

MARGARETE

   Didn't you see? I lowered my look.

FAUST

   And you forgive the liberty I took?
   What in my recent insolence when you
   Were leaving the minster I dared to do?

MARGARETE

   I was shocked. It had not happened to me before.
   No one could speak any ill of me.   3170
   Oh, I thought, is there something he could see
   That's forward and not proper in your behaviour?
   As though it seized him so he had to treat
   With the girl like that, not beat about.
   But I admit, I don't know what it was
   Began at once to stir here in your favour.
   I was angry with me, I know that much, because
   With you I could not be any angrier.

FAUST

   Sweet girl!

MARGARETE

         Let me alone.
    [*She picks a daisy and plucks the petals off it one by one.*]

FAUST

               What is that for? A bouquet?

MARGARETE

   No, no. For a game.

FAUST

           What then?

MARGARETE

               A foolish game, you'll say.   3180
    [*She plucks at the petals, murmuring to herself.*]

FAUST

   What are you whispering?

MARGARETE [*under her breath*]

             He loves me, loves me not.

FAUST
  Oh sweet, oh heavenly countenance!
MARGARETE [*continuing*]
  He loves me – not – he loves me – not . . .
    [*plucking the last petal, with a sweet joy*]
  He loves me!
FAUST
                Let what the flower says be an utterance
  Of the gods to you, child. Yes, he does love you.
  Do you know what it means that he loves you?
    [*He takes both her hands.*]
MARGARETE
  My blood runs cold.
FAUST
  Be still, be warm, and let my look,
  Let me say by the pressing of my hands to you
3190   What cannot else be said:
  To give the self up utterly and feel
  Bliss that must last for ever,
  For ever must – its end would be despair.
  No, never an end to it! No end!
    [MARGARETE *squeezes his hands, frees herself and runs
    away. He stands pensively for a moment, then follows her.*]
MARTHE [*entering*]
  Nightfall.
MEPHISTO
           And we must go.
MARTHE
  I'd bid you linger yet a while
  But this is a place so full of bile
  As if no one had anything else to do
  To pass the time away
3200   But gawp at their neighbour's every move
  And you get talked about however you behave.
  And our little pair?
MEPHISTO
           Flew up the path that way.
  Careless butterflies.

MARTHE

He seems fond of her.

MEPHISTO

And she of him. These things occur.

A Summerhouse

[MARGARETE *rushes in, hides behind the door, puts a fingertip to her lips and peeps through the crack.*]

MARGARETE

He's coming.

FAUST [*entering*]

Rascal, to tease me so!

But now . . . [*He kisses her.*]

MARGARETE [*taking hold of him and returning his kiss*]

With all my heart, my dearest, I love you.

[MEPHISTOPHELES *knocks.*]

FAUST [*stamping his foot*]

Who's there?

MEPHISTO

A friend.

FAUST

A brute!

MEPHISTO

It seems the time has come.

MARTHE [*entering*]

True, sir, it's late.

FAUST

Might I escort you home?

MARGARETE

My mother would . . . Goodbye.

FAUST

Must I be gone?

Goodbye.

MARTHE

Adieu.

MARGARETE

3210   And soon to meet again!
                              [*Exit* FAUST *and* MEPHISTOPHELES.]

MARGARETE
    Heavens above, what thoughts go on
    Inside the head of such a man!
    I'm put to shame, I stand there blushing
    And answer yes to everything.
    I'm an ignorant child, I cannot see
    What it is he sees in me.

                                   [*Exit.*]

Forest and Cavern

[FAUST *alone.*]

FAUST
    You gave me, Spirit, gave me everything
    I begged you for. Decidedly
    My way you turned your countenance in the fire.
3220   You gave me Nature in splendour for my kingdom
    And the power to feel her and enjoy her, not
    Only to visit her in cold astonishment,
    You permitted, but also granted that I see
    Into her deep heart as into a friend's heart.
    Before me you conduct the dance of all
    The living things and teach me to know myself
    Kin to the silent trees and the air and water.
    And when in the wood the stormwind roars and creaks
    And the giant fir toppling lays low
3230   And squashes the boughs and boles of neighbours
    And the hill booms and thuds with the falls,
    You lead me then to the safe cavern and show
    Me then to myself and the deep wonders, the secrets,
    Of my own heart are opened to me.
    And when on my sight the clean moon
    Rises hither, soothing, from the rock walls then,

From the damp greenery, the silver shapes
Of worlds before mine ride the air upwards
And soften the strict pleasures of contemplation.

But nothing that's perfect comes a human's way.   3240
I feel that now. With the joys that bring
Me nearer and nearer to the gods, you gave me
The companion I cannot any longer
Do without though in cold insolence
He lowers me in my own view, and one breath
Of one of his words converts your gifts to nothing.
Busily now he is fanning in my heart
A wild fire hotter for her lovely image. So
I stagger from lusting after to enjoyment
And in the enjoyment parch for the lusting after.   3250
     [*Enter* MEPHISTOPHELES.]

MEPHISTO
    Will you not soon have led this life enough?
    So going on and on, how can it please you?
    Doubtless to try it's good. But let's be off
    Again now, trying something new.

FAUST
    I wish you had other things to do
    When the day is kind than torment me.

MEPHISTO
    Indeed, I'm glad to let you rest.
    I don't need asking to by you.
    A man so rough, curmudgeonly
    And mad is not much company.   3260
    All day long I have my hands full
    And what would please Sir best or least
    By the look of him's impossible to tell.

FAUST
    Entirely typical!
    Annoys me, and wants thanks for it.

MEPHISTO
    Poor son of the earth, had you not had
    Me what life would you have led?

From all fantastical fiddle-faddle
Have I not given you a long respite?
3270 Were there no me, some while ago
Earth would have seen the back of you.
Why sit your life out like an owl
In a crack in a cliff or a sunless hole?
Why nourish yourself like the toad that sucks
On soggy moss and dripping rocks?
A fine pastime! It seems we're not
Entirely shot of the doctor yet.

FAUST

Do you understand what new life-potency
This passage in the wilds gives me?
3280 Devil as you are, if you could guess
At it, you'd not allow my happiness.

MEPHISTO

Unearthly pleasures! What suits you
Is lying on the hills in night and dew,
Embracing heaven and earth in ecstasy,
Bloating yourself up to a divinity,
Burrowing to the earth's core on a wild surmise,
Feeling in you God labouring all six days,
Enjoying I don't know what by a proud power
And into all things, blissful lover, flowing over,
3290 The son of the earth entirely rapt away,
He consummates his lofty intuition – in what way
    [*he makes a gesture*]
It would not be proper for me to say.

FAUST

How you disgust me!

MEPHISTO

                        Unpalatable?
You may well be disgusted, being so moral.
Chaste ears must never hear about
Things chaste hearts cannot do without.
But now and then by all means do amuse
Yourself by telling yourself lies.
You won't last long at it, you'll soon

Be ridden into the ground again   3300
And end, if it goes on, in dread
And mortal horror, raving mad.
Enough of this. Your sweetheart sits
Drearily at home and frets.
She loves you so, what can she do?
All she can think about is you.
Your love was a raging spate at the start,
Like a brook that swells with the melting snow
You flooded love into her heart
And now your little brook's gone shallow.   3310
I'd say instead of lording it
Among the trees Sir might see fit
To give this girl still wet behind the ears
What's due her for the love she bears.
Her time drags pitiably,
She stands at the window, watches the clouds go by
Over the old town walls and far away.
'Would I had wings', is her one song
All day long, half the night long.
Now she is cheerful, but sad mostly;   3320
Now weeping till she can weep no more;
Then calm again, apparently,
And always in love, that for sure.

FAUST
Serpent! Serpent!

MEPHISTO [*aside*]
I will have what I want.

FAUST
Get thee hence, foul thing!
Don't utter beauty's name, don't bring
The hungering thought of her sweet body
Back on my flesh that is half crazed already.

MEPHISTO
Then what's to be done? She thinks you've fled.   3330
And she's not far wrong, it must be said.

FAUST
I'm near her, far as I might be,

I can never forget her, never let her go,
I'm jealous that her lips meanwhile bestow
Their touch still on Christ's body.

MEPHISTO

Yes, I've envied you for the twins which feed
Among the lilies, friend, I have indeed.

FAUST

Pimp, get thee gone!

MEPHISTO

                I love your scolding. It makes me laugh.
God who created girls and boys
3340   Himself did forthwith recognize
The noblest calling: helping them get off.
Come now, what a song and dance you make!
You're wanted in your sweetheart's bedroom, for heaven's
    sake,
Not at the gallows, as one might suppose.

FAUST

And if in her arms I know the joys of heaven
And warm myself against her heart? What then?
Do I not feel the harm done her always?
Am I not the fugitive, the unhoused man,
The man not human, purposeless, restless,
3350   Who in the rage of lust like water overran
In roaring falls down rocks towards the abyss?
And she, her senses muffled still in girlhood,
Aside on a little Alpine meadow housing simply,
Confined in all she ever did
In the little world of domesticity.
And I, God-hated,
I could not rest
Content seizing the rocks merely
And shattering them to smithereens, I must
3360   Undermine her too, her peace.
So she is hell's demanded sacrifice.
Devil, now help me shorten the time of dread.
Let what must happen happen now,

Let her fate break around my head,
Let her come to perdition as I do.

MEPHISTO

On fire again! Back on the boil!
Go in and comfort her, you fool!
When a thinking head like yours can't spy
An outcome it thinks the end is nigh.
Life favours the brave. You already are   3370
In with the devil on many another score.
Nothing in the world disgusts me more
Than a devil in despair.

Gretchen's Room

[GRETCHEN *at the spinning wheel, alone.*]
I have no peace,
But only pain,
I'll never have peace,
Ever again.

Life without him
Is the grave to me,
The whole wide world   3380
Is a waste to me.

My poor wits
Are all astray,
My poor thinking
Is all in bits.

I have no peace,
But only pain,
I'll never have peace
Ever again.

3390   Only for him
        Do I look out,
        For no one else
        Do I leave the house.

        His lifting step,
        His noble poise,
        The smile on his lips,
        The power in his eyes

        And all his talk
        That bewitches me,
3400   How he takes my hand,
        How he kisses me.

        I have no peace,
        But only pain,
        I'll have no peace
        Ever again.

        Under my breast
        I ache to be
        Held by him
        And him by me

3410   And kissing him all
        And how I will
        And at his mouth
        Lie slaked and still.

Marthe's Garden

[MARGARETE *and* FAUST.]

MARGARETE
  Promise me, Heinrich.

FAUST
                          Whatever I can.

MARGARETE
  Say where you stand with religion.
  You are a good man through and through
  But you don't think much of religion, do you?

FAUST
  You feel I love you? Then, dear child, let be.
  For those I love I would lay down my life but leave
  In faith and feeling all men free.   3420

MARGARETE
  That isn't right. We must believe.

FAUST
  Must?

MARGARETE
          Oh if I could mend your mind! Alas
  You do not even respect the Sacraments.

FAUST
  I do.

MARGARETE
          Not as a thing that your heart wants.
  When were you last at confession or at mass?
  Do you believe in God?

FAUST
                          Dearest, who can say
  I believe in God? You may
  Ask priest or sage. Their answer
  Will only seem to mock the questioner.

MARGARETE
  So you don't believe?

FAUST
                          My sweet   3430

Look at me, hear me aright.
Who can speak his name?
Who can proclaim
Belief in him?
And who in his heart can feel
And dare say like the fool
I don't believe in him?
He comprehends all things
And holds in place all things.
3440   Does he not comprehend and hold in place
You, me, himself?
Is not the arch of heaven over us
And the firm earth under us?
And the everlasting stars do they not rise,
Friendly in aspect, over us?
Am I not looking now into your eyes
And everything rushing
To your head and to your heart
And in an everlasting mystery
3450   All weaving close, invisibly visible?
Fill your heart full of it, vast as it is,
And in that feeling coming wholly into bliss
Then call it what you will.
Call it happiness, the heart or love or God,
I have no name
For it. The feeling is all,
Names are a noise and smoke
Obscuring heaven's flame.

MARGARETE
All well and good and as it should be.
3460   The priest himself says much the same
Only a little bit differently.

FAUST
So all hearts speak
Wherever they may be under heaven's light
Each in a tongue they call their own.
Why may not I in mine?

MARGARETE

Saying it so perhaps you might get by
But all the same, it isn't right.
You have no christianity, that's why.

FAUST

Dear child.

MARGARETE

How it has troubled me
To see you in that company.

FAUST

Why so?

MARGARETE

The man you have with you,
My soul detests him through and through.
Nothing in all my born days has
Hurt my heart the way he does
With his ugly look, that man.

FAUST

My pretty thing, have no fear.

MARGARETE

It queers my blood when he is there.
Usually I like everyone
But when I'm longing to see you again
Inside I fill with dread of him
And think besides there is no good in him.
God forgive me if I'm unfair.

FAUST

Freaks like him are also necessary.

MARGARETE

I could not bear his kind around me.
We never see him in this place
Without there's mockery in his face
And some bad mood as well.
He has no part in anything, you can tell,
He cannot love a soul and that's as plain
Between his eyes as a mark of Cain.
How good I feel when you hold me,

So given up to you and warm and free,
But I close up inside when he is there.

FAUST

Angel, how prescient you are!

MARGARETE

It overwhelms me so that when
He comes and joins us, there and then
I even think I do not love you any more.
And I could never pray if he were here
And that eats into my very soul. You too,
3500   Heinrich, must feel it as I do.

FAUST

You do not like him, that's for sure.

MARGARETE

I must go now.

FAUST

                    Oh will I never
Be let to settle on your breast a while,
Drive heart in heart and soul into your soul?

MARGARETE

Oh, if only I slept alone
Gladly tonight I'd leave you the door undone.
But Mother is a shallow sleeper
And were we to be caught by her
At once it would be the death of me.

FAUST

3510   Angel, that need not happen. See
This little bottle. It would only take
Three drops in her drink to drape
Her nature sweetly in a deep sleep.

MARGARETE

What will I not do for your sake?
I hope it will not harm her though.

FAUST

Love, if it might, would I advise you so?

MARGARETE

Dearest, if I only look at you
I am driven by your will, I don't know how.

I have done so many things for you and now
There's scarcely anything left for me to do.   [*Exit.*]   3520
   [*Enter* MEPHISTOPHELES.]

MEPHISTO

Miss Nuisance! Has she gone?

FAUST

                     Spying again?

MEPHISTO

Indeed at length I listened in
On the Doctor and his catechist.
You'll feel the benefit, I trust.
Girls, after all, do like to know a man
Abides by custom and is straight and pious.
If he knuckles under there, they think, he will to us.

FAUST

Monster, it is closed to you
How this sweet soul, so true
In her belief   3530
That is to her the one way to salvation,
Inflicts upon herself a holy grief
That she must think the man she loves goes to perdition.

MEPHISTO

Supersensual sensual lover that you are,
A girl is leading you a dance.

FAUST

You misbegotten freak of filth and fire!

MEPHISTO

An expert too in the physiognomic science.
She feels when I am there she does not quite know how.
This mug of mine portends some hidden sense,
She feels for certain I'm some wayward spirit   3540
Or even the devil himself for all I know.
Well then, tonight?

FAUST

              What's that to you?

MEPHISTO

Come, come, I have much joy in it.

At the Well

[GRETCHEN *and* LIESCHEN *with their pitchers.*]

LIESCHEN
You've heard about Bärbelchen, have you?

GRETCHEN
Not a word. I don't see anybody.

LIESCHEN
Sybille said today. It's true.
She's made a fool of herself finally.
So much for her airs and graces.

GRETCHEN
Why?

LIESCHEN
It stinks.
She's nourishing two when she eats and drinks.

GRETCHEN
3550   Oh.

LIESCHEN
She had it coming and now it's come.
All that running after him!
Out walking here and there
And taken dancing everywhere
And Number One wherever
And waited on with cakes and wine
She thought her looks were extra fine,
So shameless she never blushed to take
All the gifts he cared to make.
3560   All that petting and kissing, then
Suddenly the flower's gone.

GRETCHEN
Poor thing.

LIESCHEN
You can't be sorry for her.
When the rest of us were spinning and Mother
At night wouldn't let us down the stairs

There she was with her darling boy
On the bench by the door in the dark, the hours
For him and her went sweetly by.
She'll knuckle under now, I'd say,
In her shift in church she'll rue the day.

GRETCHEN
Surely he'll marry her.   3570

LIESCHEN
He'd be a fool. A lad like he is
Can breathe fresh air in other places.
He's gone already.

GRETCHEN
                    That's not right.

LIESCHEN
But getting him won't mend her plight.
The boys will tear her garland up
And we'll strew chaff on her doorstep.

                                                    [*Exit.*]

GRETCHEN [*making her way home*]
How brave a scold I used to be
Whenever a poor girl went astray.
For the sins of others I never could
Find words enough to say how bad.   3580
I thought them black, but black as they were
Still I wished them blackened more.
I blessed my life, took pride of place,
Now sin and I are face to face.
But – everything that drove me to it,
Heavens, it was good, oh it was sweet.

Shrine in the Town Wall

[*In a niche in the wall is an image of the* Mater Dolorosa, *vases in front of it.*]

GRETCHEN [*putting fresh flowers in the vases*]
O Lady of Sorrows
Oh mercifully incline
Your countenance over this trouble of mine.

3590 Pierced through the heart
Lady of a Thousand Sorrows
To your dead son you raise your eyes

And to the Father gaze
And send up sighs
For His trouble and yours.
Who can feel
The pain
That works in my flesh and bone?
My poor heart's fears,
3600 Its trembling, its desires
Nobody knows but you alone.

Wherever I go
Oh woe and woe and woe
Here in my bosom aches.
So soon as I'm alone
I weep, weep, weep
And this heart breaks.

The pots beneath my window
I watered with my tears
3610 Early this morning, oh
When I plucked you these flowers.

The bright sun rose early
Into my room but I
Sat up in bed already
In all my misery.

From shame and death keep me
Lady of Sorrows, incline
Your countenance mercifully
On this trouble of mine.

Night

[*The street outside* GRETCHEN's *door. Her brother,*
VALENTIN, *a soldier.*]

VALENTIN

When I was in a company   3620
With drink and big talk flowing free
And my loud mates were bawling through
The pick of all the girls they knew
And slurred their praises with the tipple –
I leaned my elbows on the table
And sat at ease and listened while
The bragging talk went up and down,
And stroked my whiskers with a smile
And raised a flagon of my own
And said, 'Say what you like, but tell me   3630
Whether in all this country
There's any girl fit to undo
My darling sister Gretel's shoe.'
And drank to that and sent it round
And some bellowed, 'The man is right!
She is the flower of all her kind.'
The boasters shut up tight.
And now! Enough to tear your hair

And dash your brains out. Everywhere
3640   Any wretch with smirk and sneer
Can drag my good name in the mire
And like a bad debtor I'll sit
And every chance word make me sweat
And though I thumped them black and blue
Still I couldn't say it wasn't true.

What's that? What creeps towards me?
A pair of them, I do believe.
If he's the one I'll have him instantly.
He will not leave this place alive.

[*Enter* FAUST *and* MEPHISTOPHELES.]

FAUST

3650   There in the window of the sacristy, see how
The little flare of lamplight
Faints now aside and low
And in from all around presses the night.
It darkens in me too like that.

MEPHISTO

And I feel like the skinny tomcat
That slopes down fire escapes
And round the houses closely creeps
And pretty virtuous it makes me feel,
A bit of thievery, a bit of tail.
3660   I feel the whisper of our glorious Walpurgis Night
Through me already. It comes round again
The night after tomorrow night.
Plenty to stay awake for then!

FAUST

How near to appearing in the open air
Is the buried treasure I see glimmering over there?

MEPHISTO

You'll have the pleasure very soon
Of lifting out the pot, I'd say.
I took a squint the other day –
Some lion dollars in it, very fine.

FAUST

  Not any jewellery, not a ring   3670
  To ornament my sweetheart?

MEPHISTO

  I believe I did see such a thing –
  Pearl loops, of a sort.

FAUST

  That will do nicely. I grieve if ever
  I'm empty-handed when I go to her.

MEPHISTO

  Nonetheless you shouldn't disdain
  Enjoyment gratis now and again.
  Seeing that the heavens are bright with stars
  Let a true work of art delight your ears.
  I shall sing her a moral ditty   3680
  To bewitch her all the more completely.
    [*He sings to the zither.*]
    Sweet Kathrinchen
    Why are you here
    At your sweetheart's door
    At the first peep of the sun?
    Don't, oh don't!
    He will let you in
    A maid but you won't
    Come out a maid again.

    Beware, beware,   3690
    Once it is done
    It's goodnight then
    Poor thing, oh you poor thing.
    If you love a man
    Don't ever, don't ever
    Do the thief a favour
    Until you wear his ring.

VALENTIN [*stepping forward*]

  Damned rat-catcher, enticer on the street,
  God's blasts, who is it you want?

3700   First to the devil goes the instrument
        And the singer follows suit.

MEPHISTO
        The zither's in two, there's nothing left.

VALENTIN
        And now it'll be your skull that's cleft.

MEPHISTO [*to* FAUST]
        Professor, stand your ground. Be quick.
        Stay close, be led by me.
        Whip out your little tickling-stick.
        You thrust and I will parry.

VALENTIN
        Then parry this.

MEPHISTO
                        Indeed I will.

VALENTIN
        And this.

MEPHISTO
                Why not?

VALENTIN
                        Am I fighting the devil?
3710   What's happening? My hand is lamed.

MEPHISTO [*to* FAUST]
        Thrust now.

VALENTIN [*falling*]
                        I am hurt.

MEPHISTO
                                The lout is tamed.
        Away. We must be gone. Come quick.
        Already there's a murderous hue and cry.
        We get on famously, the police and I,
        But still a capital offence is problematic.

MARTHE [*at the window*]
        Come on out! Come out!

GRETCHEN [*at the window*]
                                Bring a light! A light!

MARTHE [*as above*]
        They quarrel, they scrap, they scream, they fight!

CROWD
  One of them's dead.
MARTHE [*coming out*]
  Have the murderers run?
GRETCHEN [*coming out*]
  Who's lying here?
CROWD
                    Your mother's son.   3720
GRETCHEN
  What a plight this is! Oh almighty God!
VALENTIN
  I am dying. That's soon said.
  And done in a little while.
  Women, why weep and wail?
  Listen to me instead. [*They all gather round him.*]
  Gretchen, see here, you are young still
  And still not very sensible.
  You've managed very ill.
  I say this now between us two:
  You are a whore so go and do   3730
  At least the whore's thing well.
GRETCHEN
  Brother! Dear God! What talk is that?
VALENTIN
  Leave God Almighty out of it.
  What's done, unfortunately, is done
  And it will go the only way it can.
  With one, in secret, you began,
  Others soon will join the queue
  And when a dozen have had you
  All the town will too.

  When first Disgrace is born   3740
  Her place of birth is secrecy,
  We keep night's curtains drawn
  Around the sight completely.
  Indeed we'd like to murder her
  But when she grows and puffs with pride

She goes even in daylight nude
And still hasn't got any lovelier.
The fouler she is to look upon
The more she seeks the light of the sun.

3750   I see a time, I do indeed,
When decent folk will cross the road
To avoid you like a corpse for fear
Of what they'd catch from you, you whore.
If ever they look you in the face
I hope the heart in you will fail.
Never come again to the altar rail,
Never again wear pretty lace
At your throat nor a chain of gold and feel
Glad of yourself at the dance but stay
3760   With beggars and cripples hidden away
In some black squat of misery
And even if God forgives you be
Cursed on earth for ever and a day.

MARTHE
Commend your soul to God's mercy.
Will you burden it more with blasphemy?

VALENTIN
You filthy female go-between
Could I lay hands on your skin and bone
All my sins would surely be
For that good deed forgiven me.

GRETCHEN
3770   Oh brother, oh the pains of hell!

VALENTIN
Leave off weeping, will you?
When you and honour said farewell
You stabbed me to the heart. Now through
The sleep of death I pass over
To God, as an honest soldier.   [*He dies.*]

Cathedral

[*A mass, organ, singing.* GRETCHEN *in a large congre-gation,* EVIL SPIRIT *behind* GRETCHEN.]

EVIL SPIRIT

Gretchen, the difference! Then
You stepped to the altar here
Still full of innocence
And babbled prayers
From a little dog-eared prayer-book   3780
Childish games
Sharing your heart with God.
Gretchen
Where are you now?
And in your heart
What wrongdoing?
Are you praying for the soul of your mother who slept for
    you
Into a long long torment?
Whose blood is that on your doorstep?
– And under your heart   3790
Is there not already a quickening, a welling up
Fearful itself and frightening you
With present foreboding?

GRETCHEN

Alas and alas!
Would I were rid of the thoughts
That cross me every way
Against me.

CHOIR

  Dies irae, dies illa
  Solvet saeclum in favilla.
  [*Sound of the organ.*]

EVIL SPIRIT

Wrath takes hold of you.   3800
The trumpet sounds.

The graves quake.
And your heart
Raised
From the quietness of ashes
Into the torment of flames
Quakes.

GRETCHEN

I wish I was not here.
It feels as though
3810   The organ takes my breath
And the singing undoes
The depths of my heart.

CHOIR

Judex ergo cum sedebit,
Quidquid latet adparebit,
Nil inultum remanebit.

GRETCHEN

I have no room!
The pillars
Hem me in,
The vaulting
3820   Presses on me. – Give me air!

EVIL SPIRIT

Hide! Sin and disgrace
Will not stay hidden.
Air? Light?
Alas for you.

CHOIR

Quid sum miser tunc dicturus?
Quem patronum rogaturus,
Cum vix justus sit securus?

EVIL SPIRIT

The blessed
Turn away their countenances from you.
3830   The pure
Shrink from reaching out their hands to you.
Alas.

CHOIR
  Quid sum miser tunc dicturus?
GRETCHEN
  Neighbour, your smelling salts!
    [*She faints.*]

Walpurgis Night

[*The Harz Mountains, near Schierke and Elend.* FAUST
and MEPHISTOPHELES.]

MEPHISTO
  Wouldn't you find a broomstick useful?
  Myself, I'd like the hardest billy-goat.
  We'll be a long time getting there this route.
FAUST
  While I'm still sprightly on my feet
  My gnarled stick here will do me very well.
  Why shorten the way? – Snailpace   3840
  Approach through the labyrinth of the valleys
  Then mounting this rock face
  From which the stream for ever leaps and fizzes
  That's the keen spice of pleasure in a path like this.
  Spring is already weaving in the birch trees
  And even the firs have begun to feel it too.
  Should it not work on our limbs likewise?
MEPHISTO
  I must say I can't feel it doing so.
  I have the winter in my body.
  I'd like to traipse through frost and snow.   3850
  How dismally and tardily
  That red imperfect slice of moon is coming up
  And gives so poor a light at every step
  You run into a rock or tree.
  I'll summon a will-o'-the-wisp, if you don't mind.
  There's one, burning very merrily.
  I say, friend, will you be so kind?

Why blaze for nothing? Come over here,
Will you, and light the way up there.

WILL-O'-THE-WISP

3860 In awe of you I hope I may
Force good behaviour on my flighty nature.
Going in zig-zags is our usual way.

MEPHISTO

Copying humans? Is that your game?
Go straight, in the devil's name,
Or I will blow the flicker of your life out.

WILL-O'-THE-WISP

You are the master of the house, I see,
And gladly I'll do whatever you ask of me.
But think, the mountain's magic-mad tonight
And if a will-o'-the-wisp must be your guiding star
3870 You can't be too particular.

FAUST, MEPHISTOPHELES, WILL-O'-THE-WISP [*in turn*]

We have entered, so it seems,
Zones of magic, zones of dreams.
Lead us, now's your chance to shine.
In the wide and desolate spaces
Bring us further forward soon.

I see trees, behind them more trees,
See them swiftly shifting by us
And the steep cliffs, see them bowing
And the rocks with their long noses –
3880 Hear them snoring, hear them blowing.

Over stones and over green
Brook and brooklet hurry down.
Is that soughing? Is that singing?
Are those love's sweet elegies,
Voices of the heavenly days?
Things we hope for, things we love!
Now returning, like the tales of
Ancient eras, comes the echo.

Hark! The owl, the screech, the oo-hu!
Nearer, nearer, peewit, jay.   3890
Each and every creature wakes.
Leggy, paunchy, through the grasses,
Newts are under way.
And the twisting roots like snakes
Out of rock and sandy places
Reach out wondrous ties and nooses
So to scare us, so to snare us,
Gross and bulbous stumps, alive,
Feel with arms of octopuses
After wayfarers. The mice   3900
Thousandfold in different dappling
Thread the heather and the moss.
And the glow-worms, wave on wave,
Flock and pack and make a muddling
Escort on the way for us.

Are we making any progress?
Seems we stand here motionless
On a hub of giddiness
While the trees and rocks pull faces
And the bloating burping mazy   3910
Jack-o'-lanterns multiply.

MEPHISTO

Take tight hold of the hem of my cloak.
Here is a sort of middle peak.
From here we see, to our astonishment,
Mammon inside the mountain, incandescent.

FAUST

How weird that glimmering through the ground
Like a bad dawn, reddish. Flickers of it
Like lightning play around
Even the deep mouths of the pit.
A puff of vapour here, drifts over there,   3920
Then a hot light shines through the veiling haze,
Creeps like a delicate thread,
Breaks forth like a well-head,

And ramifies a hundred ways
And winds a good stretch through the valley
Until in this tight corner here
It comes to a sudden single end
And sparks fly up in a spray
Like broadcast golden sand.

3930   See now: in all its height
The rock wall is alight.

MEPHISTO

Does not Sir Mammon illuminate
His palace splendidly for the feast?
Lucky you are to have seen this sight.
And now here come the guests, post haste.

FAUST

The windbride rockets through the air!
She thwacks me hard on the back of my neck!

MEPHISTO

Seize hold of the ancient ribs of the rock!
She'll tip you into the pit! Beware!

3940   Now fog thickens the night;
The forest is cracked through;
Owls start up in fright;
Columns are split in two
In the palaces of evergreen;
Boughs sigh and break;
The trunks make a vast moan;
The roots yawn and creak;
In dire muddle and smother
Things crash on one another.

3950   Down clefts of scree
The wind whips like a banshee.
Above and far and near
Voices – do you hear?
The rave, the roar
Of magic on the mountain everywhere.

CHORUS OF WITCHES

Off to the Brocken the witches troop,
The stubble is yellow, the seed is green.

In multitudes they meet again,
And Old Nick sits on the top of the heap.
Furze and furrow, brook and break,   3960
The witches fart, the billy-goats reek.

VOICE
All alone comes Mother Baubo
Mounted on a farrow-sow.

CHORUS
Honour be given where honour is due.
Make way for the Lady. Show her through.
A solid sow, bearing the Mother,
The whole tribe of witches will follow her.

VOICE
Which way did you come?

VOICE
                              By Ilsenstein.
I took a look in the owl's nest.
What big eyes!

VOICE
                              Brimstone and bane!   3970
Why ride so fast?

VOICE
She went for me with beak and claw.
See: my face is raw.

CHORUS OF WITCHES
The way is wide, the way is long
And what a bedlam throng!
Poke with a fork, thrust with a broom,
Choke the brat and bust the womb.

WARLOCKS [*half-chorus*]
We creep along like the snail in his house.
All the women are in the lead.
For when we're off to Old Nick's house   3980
Women are a thousand yards ahead.

WARLOCKS [*other half-chorus*]
That may be more or less the score:
In a thousand paces a woman is there.
But however she hurries she's always behind

The man: he's there in a leap and a bound.
VOICE [*from above*]
  Come with us from the tarn, come with us, do!
VOICES [*from below*]
  We'd like to rise to the heights with you.
  We wash and we're clean as clean can be
  But also unfruitful eternally.
BOTH CHORUSES
3990 The wind is still, the stars have fled,
  The sad moon seeks to hide her head.
  With a roar the magic chorus sends
  Sprays of sparks aloft in thousands.
VOICE [*from below*]
  Stay! Stay!
VOICE [*from above*]
  Who's calling there from the split rocks?
VOICE [*from below*]
  Take me with you! Away! Away!
  Three hundred years I've climbed already
  But cannot reach the top of the mountain.
  I want to be with my kith and kin.
BOTH CHORUSES
4000 A pole will carry you, so will a broom
  And so will a fork and a billy-goat.
  The man who can't get a lift tonight
  He never will till the end of time.
HALF-WITCH [*from below*]
  I've trotted after, many a year.
  How far the others already are!
  I cannot settle at home but here
  I get no further forward either.
CHORUS OF WITCHES
  The ointment gives the witches spirit.
  A trough will make a brave boat
4010 And a bit of rag a sail for it.
  You'll never fly if you don't tonight.
BOTH CHORUSES
  And when we turn around the peak

We skim the ground with a trailing stroke
And cover the heath far and wide
With all our witchy brood.
  [*They descend and settle.*]
MEPHISTO
  A pushing and shoving, a slipping and slapping,
  A hissing and twisting, a blowing and yapping,
  Sparks and lights and fire and stink –
  The witches' very element, don't you think?
  Stay close! We're lost as soon as blink!   4020
  Where are you?
FAUST [*in the distance*]
                  Here.
MEPHISTO
                  Dragged off so far already?
  I shall pull rank. Seems it is necessary.
  Make way! Old Harry's coming. My sweet rabble, make
      way!
  Professor, here, catch hold. And now away
  In one, out of this hurly-burly
  That is too wild even for such as me.
  Something attracts me in those bushes,
  A peculiar shining, I don't know what it is.
  Come along, let's slip in there, shall we?
FAUST
  Spirit of contradiction, lead me where you like.   4030
  Fine lot of sense it seems to make!
  We climb the Brocken on Walpurgis Night and quit
  All company nowhere special for the hell of it.
MEPHISTO
  But see the bright flames over there.
  A cheerful club has come together,
  Where two or three are gathered you are not alone.
FAUST
  I'd rather be on the top of the mountain.
  I can see curling smoke and fire.
  The crowds are hurrying to the Evil One,
  There many a riddle will be undone.   4040

MEPHISTO

And many another done up again.
Leave the great world to its roaring ways,
Here in the quiet we shall house.
It has long been traditional
In the great world to carve out the small.
I see young witches with nothing on
And old ones covered up – wisely.
Be nice will you, if only to please me.
Small trouble and any amount of fun.

4050   Hark! Instruments! Hark at their noise!
Have to get used to their damned squailing din.
Come along! Come along! It can't be otherwise.
I'll step ahead and lead you in
And I will couple you up anew.
This is no small world. What do you say, my friend?
Look, you can hardly see its end,
A hundred fires burning in a row.
Dancing and gossip, food, drink, love are here –
Tell me, can you, where there's better fare.

FAUST

4060   And how, to effect this introduction,
Will you appear – as devil or magician?

MEPHISTO

It's true, I'm very used to going incognito.
However, for a gala day you put your gongs on show.
I'm not distinguished by a garter but
There's proper honour here for my clubfoot.
Do you see the snail? Comes creeping up to us.
With her feeling seeing face
She's already had the whiff of me. Useless
To try denying myself in this place.

4070   Come now, we'll go from fire to fire as though
You came to woo and I to speak for you.
     [*To a group sitting over the dying embers of a fire*]
Gentlemen, why sit at this extreme?
Old age does better on the middle ground
With youthful high life whirling all around.

A man's enough alone in his own home.

GENERAL

Don't hope the nation will keep faith,
Don't call the debt she owes you in.
For with the people, as with women,
The favourite is always youth.

MINISTER

How far they've erred from the right road! 4080
Give me the good old men of yesterday.
When we were top, you will agree,
That was a Golden Age indeed!

PARVENU

We knew which side our bread was buttered then
And did things we should not have, frequently.
Now everything turns and turns again
Just when we wished to hold it steady.

AUTHOR

Where is there now a reader for
A work that's moderately wise?
Look at the youngsters nowadays: 4090
They know it all, like never before.

MEPHISTO [who suddenly looks very old]

I feel the people ripe for Judgement Day
And this my last climb up the witches' hill
And since my little keg is running cloudy
The world is in decline as well.

PEDLAR-WITCH

Gentlemen, don't pass me by,
Don't miss this opportunity.
Scrutinize my stock with care,
Wares of every kind are here,
Better than anywhere and more, 4100
And none among them, not a one,
That hasn't on occasion been
To men and the world a grievous bane.
There's no knife here that's not drawn blood,
Nor cup from which somebody whole and hale
Has not drunk hot corroding death, no jewel

That has not tempted and misled
Some loveable woman, nor sword that never stuck
A conned opponent in the back.

MEPHISTO

4110   Sister, you're out of touch. Things have moved on.
You trade in what has been and gone.
Get into novelties instead,
If it's not novel no one's interested.

FAUST

Must not forget myself whatever I do.
But what a market, what a show!

MEPHISTO

The whole turmoil is heading for the top,
Shoving and shoved you are carried up.

FAUST

But who is that?

MEPHISTO

                Take careful note of her:
That is Lilith.

FAUST

          Who?

MEPHISTO

                    Adam's first wife. Be sure

4120   You never fall into her beautiful hair,
The only splendour she is pleased to wear.
If it can catch her a young man
She will not quickly let him go again.

FAUST

Two sitting over there, one old, one young,
How they jigged! How they sprang!

MEPHISTO

No rest tonight. See they begin
The dance again. Come now, we must join in.

FAUST [*dancing with the* YOUNG WITCH]

Once upon a time I dreamed
A lovely dream: an apple tree,

4130   Two lovely apples, they tempted me
They shone so bright, and up I climbed.

BEAUTIFUL YOUNG WITCH
>Apples are your heart's desire,
>Even in Paradise they were.
>It tickles my delight to know
>Such apples grow in my garden too.

MEPHISTO [*dancing with the* OLD WITCH]
>Once I had a wicked dream,
>I saw a tree the lightning split,
>It had an enormous hole in it
>So big! But I liked it just the same.

OLD WITCH
>I give the best hello I can
>To Sir, the Clubfoot Gentleman.
>Keep a good bung handy by
>Unless the big hole makes you shy.

4140

PROCTOPHANTASMIST
>Damned tribe, how dare you carry on like this?
>We proved it to you long ago beyond a doubt
>That spirits never walk on normal feet,
>And now you're dancing, humanly, like us.

BEAUTIFUL YOUNG WITCH [*dancing*]
>What's that man doing at our ball?

FAUST [*dancing*]
>He pokes his nose in everywhere, that's all.
>What others dance he has to calibrate.
>If any step gets by without
>Some quatsch of his on it, he thinks it isn't one.
>What most annoys him is when we move on.
>If you went round in circles on the spot
>The way he does himself at his old mill
>At least he would approve of that
>And like it best if you'd salute him and were grateful.

4150

PROCTOPHANTASMIST
>Still there? You are very impertinent!
>Vanish, will you! This is the Enlightenment!
>The race of devils will not play by the book,
>Clever as we are, in Tegel there's still a spook.
>For years I've swept away the non-existent

4160

And still it's there. Oh very impertinent!

BEAUTIFUL YOUNG WITCH
    Since we're still here, why can't you let us be?

PROCTOPHANTASMIST
    I tell you spirits candidly
    I will not tolerate your tyranny.
    The one who gives the orders here is me –
        [*the dancing continues*]
    Except tonight. Tonight I labour in vain.
    But I will write another travel book at least
4170   And hope before my spirit gives up the ghost
    To make the devils and the poets toe the line.

MEPHISTO
    He'll find a puddle to sit down in now.
    He needs relief – and that is how.
    And while the leeches are enjoying his behind
    The spirits will evacuate his mind.
        [*To* FAUST *who has quitted the dance*]
    Why let the girl go, she was beautiful
    And sang to you so sweetly in the dance?

FAUST
    A little red mouse sprang
    Out of her mouth in the midst of her song.

MEPHISTO
4180   So what? No need to take offence.
    Why should that make a lover turn away?
    Be glad the little mouse was red not grey.

FAUST
    Then I saw . . .

MEPHISTO
                    What?

FAUST
                            Mephisto, do you see
    That beautiful pale child alone out there?
    She goes with such slow difficulty
    As though her feet were tied together.
    She seems to me, I must confess,
    My poor Gretchen's likeness.

MEPHISTO

Leave that. No one who goes with that will thrive.
It is a magic image, an idol, not alive.   4190
A meeting with it is not good,
The set look stops a human's blood,
It turns a man almost to stone.
You've heard of the Medusa, I suppose?

FAUST

Truly, she has the look of one
Dead and no loving hand will close her eyes.
That is the breast that Gretchen showed
For me and that sweet body I enjoyed.

MEPHISTO

Fool easily misled, that is the magic art.
She seems to every man his own sweetheart.   4200

FAUST

What bliss it is! What agony!
I cannot leave her looking so at me.
How strange that she should decorate
Her lovely throat
With a sole red loop no broader than
The back of a knife.

MEPHISTO

                        I see it too. She can
Carry her head under her arm as well
Since Perseus chopped it off for her. –
How you do lust to be deluded still!
Come now, towards that little hill,   4210
Such fun! It's like the Prater here
And unless someone's deceiving me
In truth I see a real theatre.
What is this then?

SERVIBILIS

                        Just beginning again,
A new piece, the last of seven.
It's usual here to show so many,
Written by a dilettante,
Acted by dilettanti too.

Pardon me, gentlemen, if I disappear
4220   To raise the curtain, dilettantily.

MEPHISTO
How right that I should find you here:
The Blocksberg is the place for you.

Walpurgis Night's Dream
Or
The Golden Wedding of Oberon and Titania
An Intermezzo

STAGE MANAGER
Tonight for once the doughty sons
Of Mieding will take it easy.
An old hill, a sodden dale,
These will be all our scenery.

HERALD
It is a golden wedding
When half a century's through.
If they give over rowing
That golden will do.

4230
OBERON
Spirits, if you are present here
Make all the show you can.
Oberon and Titania
Are best of friends again.

PUCK
When Puck arrives and tricks and turns
And flicks his dancing feet
A hundred follow after him
Not to miss the treat.

ARIEL
Ariel moves the song along
4240   In the pure tones of heaven.
He lures abundant ugly mugs
But also pretty women.

OBERON

> Man and wife can learn from us
> The art of getting on.
> Two supposed to love, tell them:
> Try separation.

TITANIA

> The man who sulks, the wife who moods,
> Quickly seize hold of them.
> Send her towards Antarctica
> And to the North Pole him.

FULL ORCHESTRA [*fortissimo*]

> Blue-Tail Fly and Bluebottle,
> Them and their relations
> Frog on a Log and Grasshopper Green:
> They are the musicians.

SOLO

> And who comes here? The Bagpipes does.
> It is a soap bubble.
> Hark at the drawling twaddle-twaddle
> Through its flattened schnozzle.

SPIRIT IN THE MAKING

> A spider's feet, a toad belly
> And wings to the little thing!
> Even before the beastie's there
> It's started versifying.

PAIR OF LOVERS

> Stepping small and leaping high
> Through scents and honeydew.
> Footing it so is nice enough
> But nicer if we flew.

CURIOUS TRAVELLER

> Is this some mocking masquerade?
> Can I believe my eyes?
> Is Oberon, the lovely god,
> Still visible nowadays?

THE VOICE OF ORTHODOXY

> He has no claws, he has no tail
> But still, even without,

4250

4260

4270

Like the gods of Ancient Greece he is
A devil beyond a doubt.

NORTHERN ARTIST

As yet whenever I grasp a thing
I do so sketchily,
But I'm preparing early for
My trip to Italy.

PURIST

Alas, my bad luck brings me here
4280   Among the morally slipshod.
Of all the witches only two
Have powdered where they should.

YOUNG WITCH

Powder is, like any dress,
For grey old women. Astride
My billy-goat I show you all
How good a girl looks nude.

MATRON

Good manners will not permit me
To scold you on the spot.
I hope, however, that young and sweet
4290   As you are now, you'll rot.

CONDUCTOR

Bluebottle and Blue-Tail Fly,
Leave the naked girl alone.
And keep in time, Frog on a Log,
And you, Grasshopper Green.

WEATHERVANE [*veering one way*]

What excellent company this is!
Young women wherever you look
And young men too and one and all
The hopefullest of folk.
[*Veering the other way*]
And unless the maw of Mother Earth
4300   Gapes and they vanish in it,
With a run and a jump I'll post myself
To hell this very minute.

XENIA

> As insects we are here tonight
> With tiny sharpened shears
> To honour Satan, our papa,
> As piety requires.

HENNINGS

> See how they congregate and jest
> And jostle in a pretty throng.
> Next thing we know they'll even say
> They meant well all along.   4310

LEADER OF THE MUSES

> I'm more than glad to lose myself
> In swarms of witches here.
> They might indeed be biddable.
> The Muses never were.

SOMETIME SPIRIT OF THE AGE

> It's who you know, not what you know.
> Take hold of my coat-tails, up!
> The Blocksberg has, like Germany's
> Parnassus, room at the top.

CURIOUS TRAVELLER

> Tell me the name of that stiff man?
> He walks on very proud feet   4320
> And sniffs and snuffles for all he's worth:
> 'He smells a Jesuit.'

CRANE

> I like fishing in clear waters
> And in muddy waters too.
> So, though a pious man, not even
> Devils do I eschew.

WORLDLING

> Yes, for the pious, believe me,
> All's a vehicle.
> Here on the Blocksberg they have formed
> Many a conventicle.   4330

DANCER

> Is that a new choir on the way?

I hear a distant drumming.
Easy! It's bitterns in the reeds
Unisonly booming.

DANCING MASTER

How one and all they lift their legs!
What shots at it they make!
The hunchback leaps, the fat man hops,
And don't mind how they look.

FIDDLER

Rabble! They hate one another's guts,
4340   They'd cut one another's throats.
The Bagpipes gathers them together
As Orpheus did the brutes.

DOGMATIST

I shan't be muddled by a din
Of criticism and cavils.
The Devil must exist. How else,
I ask you, could there be devils?

IDEALIST

Imagination in my mind
Is tyrannous tonight.
Truly, if I am everything
4350   Out there, I'm mad all right.

REALIST

Existence is a pain to me,
Vexes me more and more.
For the first time in my life I find
My footing not secure.

SUPERNATURALIST

I am with the greatest pleasure here,
Enjoy myself as they do.
I take the devils to be a proof
That good spirits exist too.

SCEPTIC

They follow the ignis fatuus
4360   And think the grail is near.
Doubt and cavil go with the Devil.
I'm quite at home here.

CONDUCTOR
> Frog on a Log and Grasshopper Green,
> You call that music, do you?
> Bluebottle and Blue-Tail Fly,
> Damned dilettanti crew!

THE CRAFTY
> Sanssouci is where the host
> Of creatures merrily dwell.
> We can't go on our feet any more
> So on our heads we shall.

4370

THE HELPLESS
> We wheedled titbits in the past
> But what shall we do now?
> We danced attendance everywhere
> Until our soles were through.

WILL-O'-THE-WISPS
> Out of the bog we have arrived
> And that's where we began.
> But now we're tripping in the dance
> We are the ladies' men.

SHOOTING STAR
> Out of the heights I hurtled here
> In star- and fiery light.
> Now I lie in the grass awry.
> Who'll help me to my feet?

4380

THE HEAVYWEIGHTS
> Make way, make room, make lots of space!
> The grass is trodden flat.
> Spirits are coming, but spirits who
> Materialized in fat.

PUCK
> Slim down your entry, come less like
> Baby elephants.
> Let Puck himself, the joker, stage
> The heaviest events.

4390

ARIEL
> If loving Nature or the mind
> Has given you wings, come now.

To the hill of roses I'll unwind
An airy clue for you.
ORCHESTRA [*pianissimo*]
The train of clouds, the veil of mist
Uppermost brighten.
Air in the leaves, wind in the reeds,
All goes to motes again.

Black Day. Field

FAUST

In misery! In despair! A long time pitifully wandering the earth and now a prisoner! The sweet unhappy girl, jailed as a malefactor and facing hideous torments! So she has come to that! – And you, the traitor, the good-for-nothing demon, you kept it secret! – And you stand there! You roll the devilish eyes in your head! Oh what malice! There you stand, an unbearable affront! – And she is a prisoner! In a misery never to be undone! Given over to evil demons and the judgement of unfeeling human beings! And all the while you were lulling me in tasteless distractions, hiding her greater and greater wretchedness from me and letting her go helplessly to ruin.

MEPHISTO

She's not the first.

FAUST

Dog! Abominable monster! – O infinite Spirit, transform this worm back into its dog-shape, back the way he liked to come at nights and dance in front of me or roll under the feet of harmless wayfarers and hang upon their shoulders when they fell. Change him back into his favourite form so he can crawl on his belly in the dirt before me and I can trample him for his depravity! – Not the first! – Oh grief, such grief, beyond the comprehension of any human soul, that more than one creature should ever have sunk into such deep misery, that the first herself, writhing in her mortal need, did not suffice for all the rest in the eyes of Eternal Forgiveness! She, that one, invades the very marrow of my life – and you grin calmly over the fate of thousands.

MEPHISTO

So here we are at our wits' end again. Losing your senses. Why do you humans associate with us if you can't carry it through? You wish to fly – but have no head for heights? Did we force ourselves on you or you on us?

FAUST

Stop grinning at me like that. Hungry, are you? It sickens me. – O Spirit of strength and splendour, you condescended to appear to me, you know the heart and soul of me, why did you fetter me in shame to this creature who gloats on harm and smacks his lips at ruin?

MEPHISTO

Have you finished?

FAUST

Save her or woe betide you. My uttermost curse on you for thousands upon thousands of years!

MEPHISTO

I can't undo the Avenger's locks and bonds. – Save her! – Who thrust her into her ruin, me or you? [FAUST *looks about him wildly*.] Are you reaching for the thunder? A mercy you wretched mortals were never given it. Smash to pieces whoever happens to be innocently in your way. Typical tyrant manners! In trouble? Lash out!

FAUST

Take me there! She must be freed.

MEPHISTO

And the risk you run? There's blood-guilt on the town still, of your doing. The spirits of vengeance hover where the dead man died. They await his murderer's return.

FAUST

Must I hear that from you as well? A world of murder and death on you, you monster. Take me there, I say, and free her.

MEPHISTO

I'll bring you there, and this is what I can do. Is all power

given unto me in heaven and in earth? I'll cloud the jailer's
senses, you get possession of the keys and lead her out by
human hand. I'll keep watch. The magic horses will be
ready and waiting. I'll carry the two of you off. So much I
can do.

FAUST

Away then!

Night. Open Field

[FAUST *and* MEPHISTOPHELES *arrive like the wind on*
black horses.]

FAUST

What work are they at round the Raven Stone?

MEPHISTO

4400   Don't know what they're mulling and making.

FAUST

They soar, they swoop, they settle, they hunch.

MEPHISTO

A coven of witches.

FAUST

They sprinkle and spell.

MEPHISTO

Ride on! Ride on!

Prison

[FAUST, *with a bunch of keys and a lamp, at a little iron*
door.]

FAUST

So long unused to it, the cold of all
Humanity's misery pierces me again.
She has her dwelling behind this damp wall
And her crime was a good illusion.

You shrink from going in to her,
You are afraid of seeing her again.   4410
Do it! While you dally, Death comes nearer.
    [*He seizes the lock.*]
MARGARETE [*heard singing within*]
    My mother, the whore,
    She murdered me.
    My father, the rogue,
    He supped on me.
    My little sister
    Gathered my bones
    Safe in the shade.
    Then I was a pretty bird in the glades.
    Fly away! Fly away!   4420
FAUST [*unlocking the door*]
    She does not know that her beloved listens
    And hears the rustling straw, the rattling chains.
    [*He goes in.*]
MARGARETE [*cowering away on her straw*]
    Oh they are coming! Oh Death's a bitter meal!
FAUST [*softly*]
    Hush, hush. I come with your escape.
MARGARETE [*dragging herself towards him*]
    If you are human, feel the pain I feel.
FAUST
    You will scream the jailers from their sleep.
    [*He seizes the chains, to unlock them.*]
MARGARETE [*on her knees*]
    Who gave you might and right,
    Axeman, over me?
    You come to fetch me? It is only midnight.
    Have mercy, let me be.   4430
    Until tomorrow morning, is that too long?
    [*She gets to her feet.*]
    I am so young, still so young,
    And must I die already?
    I was beautiful too, that was my bane.
    My friend was near, now he is far away,

The garland torn, the flowers strewn.
Don't lay such violent hands on me.
What have I done to you? Have pity.
Don't let me plead in vain.

4440   I never saw you in my life till now.

FAUST
Will I overlive this sorrow?

MARGARETE
Now I am wholly under your might.
First let me feed my baby again.
I cuddled him all through the night.
They took him away, to give me pain,
And now they say I murdered him.
And I will never be happy again.
They are singing songs about me. How unkind of them.
An old tale ends that way.

4450   But what it means, who are they to say?

FAUST [*throwing himself down*]
A loving man lies here who will undo
The misery fettering you.

MARGARETE [*kneeling by him*]
Oh let us kneel, let us implore
The saints! Below this threshold, see
Down these steps, see where
Hell heaves
And the Fiend
Rackets and raves
In wrath at me!

FAUST [*loudly*]

4460   Gretchen! Gretchen!

MARGARETE [*hearkening*]
That was the voice of my beloved friend!
   [*She leaps up. Her chains fall away.*]
Where is he? I heard him call. I'm free.
Let nobody deny it me.
Into his arms I will fly!
On his breast I will lie!

He called: Gretchen! He stood on the threshold.
Through the weeping and gnashing of hell,
Through the jeering and wrath of the devils he called
In the sweet loving voice that I know well.

FAUST
I am here!

MARGARETE
          You are here! Oh say so again!   4470
  [*She seizes hold of him.*]
Here! Oh he is here! He ends my agony
Of chains and terror in the dungeon!
It's you! And you have come to save me.
I am saved! –
The street is there again already
That I first saw you on
And the cheerful garden too
Where I and Marthe waited for you.

FAUST [*striving to leave*]
Come with me! Come now!

MARGARETE
                      Oh stay!
Wherever you are, there I like to be.   4480
  [*She caresses him.*]

FAUST
Hurry! Away!
If you will not hurry
It will go very ill with us.

MARGARETE
Is that all you can kiss?
My friend, so short a while away from me
And have forgotten how to kiss?
Why am I fearful reaching up to you
When from your words and looks not long ago
All of heaven poured in over me
And you kissed me as though   4490
To stop my breath? Kiss me
Or I'll kiss you. [*She embraces him.*]

Oh your lips are cold,
You say nothing.
Where can your loving
Be?
Who lost it me? [*She turns away from him.*]

FAUST

Come with me now. Sweetheart, be bold.
I'll warm you in my love a thousandfold.

4500 But follow me now. I beg for nothing more.

MARGARETE [*turning to him*]

And is it really you? Is it you for sure?

FAUST

For sure. Come now.

MARGARETE

                              And you unchain
And take me into your lap again.
How is it you do not shy away from me?
And do you know, my friend, who you are setting free?

FAUST

Hurry. Already the black of night has paled.

MARGARETE

I have killed my mother,
I have drowned my child.
Was he not given as our gift to one another?

4510 To you also. – Hard to believe it's true.
Give me your hand. I am not dreaming you.
Your beloved hand. – But oh it is wet.
Wipe it. There seems to be
Blood on it.
Oh God, what have you done!
Sheathe your sword. Oh do,
I beg you to.

FAUST

Leave that! What's done is done.
You are killing me.

MARGARETE

4520 Ah no, you must remain.
I will describe the graves to you.

You must see to them soon:
Tomorrow.
The best place give my mother
And next to her my brother,
Me a little to one side
But not too far away
And the little one on my right breast.
Nobody else will lie with me.
When I lay close and closer by your side   4530
That was a sweet and precious happiness.
But now I cannot any more. As though
I have to force myself to you
And you push me away. Nevertheless
It's you and there is kindness in your face.

FAUST

If you feel that it is me, leave this place.

MARGARETE

And go out there?

FAUST

Outside and free.

MARGARETE

                    If the grave's out there,
If death is lying in wait, then let us go.
From here to a bed where sleep will never end   4540
And not a step beyond –
Are you going now? Oh Heinrich, if I could too!

FAUST

You can. The door is open. Wish it and you are free!

MARGARETE

I cannot leave. There is no hope for me.
What good is flight? They will be lying in wait.
Wretched, to be a beggar. Worse,
A beggar under a conscience curse.
Wretched, to wander far from home,
And they will catch me all the same.

FAUST

I will not leave you.   4550

MARGARETE
   Be quick! Be quick!
   Save your poor child!
   Hurry! Climb
   The path by the stream
   And over the bridge
   And into the trees.
   Left, by the fence,
   In the pond, there.
   Catch him. He
4560   Won't stay under,
   He's kicking still.
   Save him! Save him!

FAUST
   Still, be still!
   One step and you are free.

MARGARETE
   If only we were past the hill.
   My mother sits there on a stone.
   A cold thing takes me by the hair!
   My mother sits there on a stone
   And waggles her head.
4570   Not a wave, not a nod, her head is heavy for her.
   She slept so long, she'll sleep for ever.
   She slept for our pleasure.
   Happy times we had!

FAUST
   However I plead, whatever I say
   It does no good. I must carry you away.

MARGARETE
   Let me alone! I'll not be forced.
   Don't lay your hands on me so murderously!
   All I did for you I did it lovingly.

FAUST
   Grey daylight! Sweetheart! Sweetheart!

MARGARETE
4580   Daylight! Day! The last day enters in.

My wedding day it should have been.
Tell no one you were with Gretchen already.
Alas for my garland.
Alas for what happened.
We shall see each other again
But not at the dance.
The multitude presses, silently.
Too many there are
In the streets and the square.
They toll the bell, they snap the white wand.   4590
And now they bind me, they grasp me
And haul me to the block.
And the blade that rises for mine
Rises for every neck.
The world lies dumb as the grave.

FAUST

Why was I born? I curse the day!

MEPHISTO [*appearing outside*]

You perish together if you delay.
You dither for nothing, tarry and chat.
My horses shudder at
The breaking day.   4600

MARGARETE

What thing is that breaking the earth's surface?
Him! Him! Send him away!
What does he want in the holy place?
He wants me.

FAUST

                    Live! I wish you to.

MARGARETE

Court of God, I give myself up to you!

MEPHISTO [*to* FAUST]

Come, come away. Or I leave you lost with her.

MARGARETE

Oh I am yours, oh save me, Father!
Oh angels, blessed company,
Encamp around. Have me in your care.

4610   Heinrich, you ice my blood with fear.
MEPHISTO
    She is judged.
VOICE [*from above*]
                    Is saved.
MEPHISTO [*to* FAUST]
                        Come here to me!
                            [*He disappears with* FAUST.]
    VOICE [*from within, fading*]
        Heinrich! Heinrich!

Notes

DEDICATION

This poem, in the eight-line stanzas known as *ottava rima*, was composed 24 June 1797 when Goethe took up work on *Faust* again. He placed it as the first of the three prefaces to complete *Part I*. The passivity is remarkable; the old material comes back upon him, he suffers its visitation. Strata of the poet's life, strata and mode of composition, are the subject, more than *Faust* and its particular problems. In the first publication (1808), line 21 reads, 'Mein *Leid* ertönt der unbekannten Menge...' Goethe noted that *Leid* (sorrow) was a misprint for *Lied* (song), but let it stand in later editions during his lifetime. It makes sense, of course. My translation of lines 21–3 effectively reads the word as *Lied*.

PRELUDE IN THE THEATRE

Written between 1795 and 1800 and most likely in the summer of 1797; but, since nothing in it specifically refers to *Faust*, Goethe had perhaps intended it for his own continuation of Mozart's *Magic Flute*, or for the reopening of the Weimar Court Theatre in 1798. The fourth-century Indian play *Śakuntalā*, which Goethe admired (in a translation of 1791), has a similar prelude. In so far as Goethe's prelude has to do with *Faust* the three characters may parody the Lord, Faust and Mephistopheles in the scene that follows.

220–21 *You say you're poets ... orders are*: Goethe quotes these lines in a letter to Humboldt (1 December 1831) describing how he managed to finish *Faust*.

PROLOGUE IN HEAVEN

Written probably in the summer of 1797 and certainly not later than April 1798. Based on Job 1:6–12, where God permits Satan to tempt

Job. See Introduction pp. xxxii–xxxvi on the sense this Prologue lends
to the action of the play and on Mephistopheles's function in the divine
economy. His name, of uncertain meaning, goes back through Marlowe
to the earliest chapbooks. Marlowe, following his sources, spells it
Mephostophiles.

299 *my servant*: See Job 1:8.

312 *What do you wager*: This wager between Mephisto and the Lord
     prefigures that between Mephisto and Faust.

335 *Cousin Serpent*: The temptress serpent in Genesis 3.

339 *rogue*: The German word is *Schalk*. This, and Mephisto's own
     characterization of himself (1641) as 'not one of the great', signifi-
     cantly reduces his status in the cosmic order.

THE FIRST PART OF THE TRAGEDY

Urfaust begins here. Roughly half this scene – to line 605 – belongs to the
earliest stratum (1772–5) of Goethe's work on the play. In traditional
fashion, following Marlowe and the puppet theatre, he introduces Faust
sick of learning.

Night

354–60 *Philosophy ... Law ... Physic ... Divinity ... Doctor*: Faust
       has studied in the four traditional faculties of the medieval uni-
       versity, to the highest level.

420 *Nostradamus*: Michel de Nostredame (1503–66), French astrol-
     oger and physician, published books of prophecies but no book of
     magic. Faust is here supposed to own a manuscript.

429 *the Sign of the Macrocosm*: 'The "great world" or universe, in
     contradistinction to the "little world" or microcosm, i.e. to man as
     viewed as an epitome of the universe' (*Oxford English Dictionary*,
     henceforth *OED*). The important thing here is the dynamic inter-
     connection between the two.

447–53 *How everything ... the All*: Like Jacob's dream of the ladder
       between heaven and earth (Genesis 28:12), amplified by Franciscus
       Mercurius van Helmont (1691), who was one of Goethe's sources
       in alchemy and mystical theosophy.

461 *Earth Spirit*: In *Urfaust* Goethe described the Spirit's appearance
     as repulsive (*widerlich*), but later thought of him as majestic, like
     Apollo or Jupiter. His nature and function are by no means constant.
     Rather, they change through the phases of *Faust*'s composition.

490 *Übermensch*: The word means 'Superman'. It was given notorious
     currency by Nietzsche.

518 *Famulus*: 'An attendant; esp. on a scholar or a magician' (*OED*).
     He was called Wagner in the earliest sources. Through him the
     young Goethe satirized the complacent academic learning of his
     own day and age.

606 Here began the so-called 'great lacuna' in the composition of *Faust*.
     Goethe filled the latter part of it (1770–1867) in the years 1788–
     90, and the former (606–1769) in 1798–1801.

644–51 These lines anticipate the scene at the end of *Faust, Part II*
     (11385 ff.) in which Faust is breathed upon and blinded by a figure
     personifying anxiety and care. Goethe drafted that scene and wrote
     these lines roughly at the same time, around 1800.

702 *chariot of fire*: Alludes to Elijah's ascent into heaven (2 Kings 2:11)
     but perhaps also to Phaethon's catastrophic handling of the chariot
     of the sun.

737 *Christ the Lord is risen again*: The choirs allude closely to the
     gospel accounts of Christ's resurrection. See Matthew 28, Mark
     16, Luke 24, John 20.

Outside the Town

878 *Saint Andrew's eve*: 29 November, the evening before St Andrew's
     Day itself.

949–80 These verses were written in the early 1780s, not for *Faust*.
     They are sung and danced to in Goethe's novel *Wilhelm Meister*
     (Book II, ch. 11); but there the narrator declines to pass on more
     than the first line, for fear the reader may find the rest tasteless or
     indecent.

1042–8 *There ... medicine*: Faust describes a typical alchemical pro-
     cedure: the 'marrying' of a reddish mercuric oxide (the 'Scarlet
     Lion') with a white hydrochloric acid (the 'Lily'), to produce an
     iridescent deposit (the 'Young Queen') for use against the plague.

1147 *black dog*: In the legend Faust had a familiar black dog by the
     name of Prestigiar; but it was Goethe's idea to have Mephistopheles
     appear in canine shape.

Faust's Study (I)

Probably written in April 1800; 'Faust's Study (II)' has work in it from
all three phases of *Part I*'s composition. There is a hiatus between the
two scenes which Goethe intended to bridge with another showing Faust
and Mephisto in public disputation (1712 may refer to it).

1224 *'In the beginning was the Word'*: John 1:1. Faust is interrupted in
     his translation by the poodle Mephisto, as Luther was in his by the
     Devil.

1258 *The Key of Solomon*: *Clavicula Salomonis*, a book of magic chants and spells, well known in the sixteenth century, still being used in the eighteenth.

1272 *the spell of the four*: Faust first conjures with the four elements: fire (salamander), water (undine), air (sylph), earth (goblin and incubus); then, at 1300, with the crucifix; and finally, at 1319, with the sign of the Trinity.

1334 *Lord of the Flies, Destroyer, Liar*: Translations of three of the Devil's traditional names: Beelzebub, Apollyon, Diabolus.

1396 *pentagram*: The pentagram (or witch's foot) is a five-pointed star whose lines, for magical purposes, should be drawn continuously, leaving no gaps. The one drawn here on Faust's threshold has a gap, facing out, through which Mephisto, as poodle, could get in; but the angles now facing him are tight and prevent his exit until, at 1524, the rats gnaw him an opening.

Faust's Study (II)

1535 *Junker*: A young German nobleman, especially of Prussia.

1656-9 *I bind myself . . . the same for me*: The traditional pact, which Faust treats very lightly. More important, in his view, is the wager, which he offers at 1698. For a full discussion of pact and wager see Introduction, pp. xxxii–xxxv.

1739 *The foolery . . . can go ahead*: A very trivializing compliance (by Goethe and Faust) with a requirement which, like the pact itself, is of fundamental importance in the traditional story.

1741-69 With these lines, Goethe, in 1800-1801, attached this scene to the part of it already published ten years earlier in *Faust. A Fragment*.

1868 Here Goethe reconnects his text with the *Urfaust* material and continues the satire of academic learning begun in the exchanges between Faust and Wagner. Mephisto speaks for Goethe, as he will do quite frequently throughout the play.

1913 *Scotch boots*: The German is *spanische Stiefeln*, 'Spanish boots'. They, like Scotch boots, were an instrument of torture.

1940 *encheiresis naturae*: The two words, Greek + Latin, mean 'an intervention by the hand of nature' and were used by Goethe's chemistry professor in Strasbourg as a pompous pseudo-definition of life.

2000 *Not one jot . . . abated*: Matthew 5:18: 'Till heaven and earth pass [away], one jot or one tittle shall in no wise pass from the law, till all be fulfilled.' Goethe may be alluding satirically to the Council of Nicea, AD 325, where, in the attempt to define the nature of

Christ, the Church divided over two Greek words ὁμοούσιος and ὁμοιούσιος, which are distinguished by one letter, the iota.

2048 *Eritus sicut Deus . . . malum*: The words of the Serpent to Eve in Eden, Genesis 3:5: 'ye shall be as gods, knowing good and evil.'

2070–71 *Up from the earth . . . if we're light*: Alludes to early ascents by hot-air balloon, the first by the Montgolfier brothers in 1783.

2072 *vita nuova*: Italian, 'new life'. This is my translation of the words *neuer Lebenslauf* and alludes ironically to Dante's *Vita nuova*.

Auerbach's Cellar in Leipzig

This scene is *Urfaust* material, versified and otherwise reworked for the publication of the *Fragment* in 1790. Auerbach's Cellar in Leipzig was well known to Goethe from his student days. It had seventeenth-century murals showing scenes from the life of Faust.

2090–91 *Holy Roman Empire . . . fall apart*: The Holy Roman Empire, founded in 962, had long been ramshackle and ridiculous. Napoleon ended it in 1806.

2098–2100 *We shall elect . . . your way*: Students would elect their best drinker as king or pope for the evening. But the lines also allude to the requirement, after the debacle of Pope Joan, that every new pope prove his sex.

2113 *Blocksberg*: The Brocken, in the Harz Mountains, scene of the Walpurgis Night revels. See note to 'Walpurgis Night' below.

2129 *Martin Luther*: Luther visited Leipzig in 1525, a year after Faust is said to have.

2172 *A little Paris*: Leipzig had this pretension when Goethe was a student there.

2184 *He limps as he goes*: Mephisto's cloven foot, alluded to again at 2490, 4065 and 4141.

2189–90 *Rippach . . . Hans Arse*: Rippach is a village near Leipzig. Its publican, in Goethe's student days, was called Hans Ars, which easily became Hans *Arsch*.

2262 *I offer a choice*: This magic, like Faust's riding away on a barrel (2330), is in the original chapbook.

Witch's Kitchen

This scene, written incongruously enough in the garden of the Villa Borghese in Rome in the spring of 1788, makes a sort of prologue to the Gretchen tragedy. (Faust is rejuvenated, he sees a vision of female beauty in a magic mirror.) For the setting and for its images of human folly Goethe may have had paintings by Brueghel and Teniers in mind.

I have used the old word 'meerkat' for the Witch's familiar creatures though translators generally prefer 'marmoset', 'monkey' or 'baboon'.

2401 *the lottery*: Popular in eighteenth-century Italy and France, the lottery serves here also as a pointer towards the precarious and dubious finances of that latter country just before the Revolution. In this scene and elsewhere Goethe makes a good deal of critical reference to contemporary politics.

2416 *sieve*: According to popular superstition you might sieve good from bad in human character too.

2430 *O heavenly image*: Giorgione's *Sleeping Venus* in Dresden or Titian's *Venus of Urbino* in Florence may come to mind.

2452 SD *They handle the crown carelessly*: Mephisto presides like a Lord of Misrule over the careless handling of a crown – again Goethe may be glancing at France.

2552 *times-table*: David Luke, p. 160, suggests that the Witch's times-table may be set down in a magic square 'in which each of the six horizontal and vertical lines of figures adds up to 15'.

2560–62 *to put ... the truth about*: Mephisto/Goethe mocking the Doctrine of the Trinity.

2590 *Walpurgis Night*: See note to 'Walpurgis Night' below.

2603–4 *see Helen ... in every woman*: Cf. *A Midsummer Night's Dream*, V.1.10–11: 'The lover .../ Sees Helen's beauty in a brow of Egypt.' The image in the magic mirror prefigures both Gretchen and, in *Part II*, Helen of Troy.

Street

At this point Goethe resumes the old *Urfaust* material, of which the Gretchen tragedy was the core. He gives his heroine her full name, Margarete, in his stage and dialogue directions in all the scenes (except 'Gretchen's Room') before she is seduced and in the last. Otherwise he uses the diminutive, Gretchen; and thus (or with the variants 'Margretlein' or 'Gretelchen') she is addressed or referred to by other characters. The diminutive form, like that of other girls' names, could, in Goethe's day, suggest a sexual familiarity.

Evening

2759 *Thule*: The ancient Greek and Latin name for a land six days' sail north of Britain, supposed to be the most northerly region in the world. Gretchen sings of what she subconsciously hopes for and will not get: faithful love. There is a suggestive connection with Desdemona's singing as she undresses in *Othello*, IV.3.39.

Promenade

2835 *Who overcometh shall inherit*: Revelation 2:17: 'To him that overcometh will I give to eat of the hidden manna'; and 21:7: 'He that overcometh shall inherit all things.'

At the Neighbour's House

2883–4 *I can't be seen . . . in them*: Eighteenth-century sumptuary laws (laws governing expenditure on diet and dress) strictly regulated what jewellery middle- and lower-class girls and women might wear.

2906 *takes you for a fine lady*: Mephisto, like Faust at 2605, deliberately enhances Gretchen's social class.

2983–4 *She showed him such love . . . till the last unction*: That is, she gave him syphilis, *le mal de Naples*.

Street

3037 *Sancta simplicitas!*: 'Holy simplicity!' Said to be the dying words of the martyr Jan Hus when he saw an old woman eagerly adding wood to his pyre.

Garden

3156 *virtuous wife . . . rubies*: Proverbs 31:10: 'Who can find a virtuous woman? for her price is far above rubies.'

Forest and Cavern

All of this scene, except 3342–69, was written during the second phase of work on *Faust* and published in *Faust. A Fragment* but there placed after 'At the Well'; that is, *after* Gretchen's seduction. In 1808 it was given its present position, where some of it, being now *before* Faust seduces her, does not fit. The Spirit addressed at 3217 is the Earth Spirit of 460 ff. The statement (at 3243) that he gave Mephistopheles to Faust is overridden by the 'Prologue in Heaven' (written ten years later), but Goethe left in this inconsistency also.

3326 *Get thee hence, foul thing!*: Like Christ tempted: 'Get thee hence, Satan' (Matthew 4:10).

3335–6 *twins . . . lilies*: Song of Solomon 4:5: 'Thy two breasts are like two young roes that are twins, which feed among the lilies.'

3342–69 These lines were in *Urfaust* (after the scene in the cathedral), as a speech of remorse very late in Gretchen's tragedy. In 1790 (*Fragment*) Goethe retrieved them into 'Forest and Cavern', still after her seduction; in 1808 (*Faust, Part I*) into their present position.

Gretchen's Room

Often set to music, most hauntingly by Schubert, Gretchen's verses are a spoken soliloquy, not a song.

Marthe's Garden

3414 *Heinrich*: The historical Faust was called Georg; the Faust in legend, Johann. Goethe may intend us to think that his Faust assumes the name Heinrich for deception in the love-affair. Gretchen never knows who he is.

3490 *mark of Cain*: Cain was the eldest son of Adam. He murdered his brother Abel. God set a mark upon him. The story is told in Genesis 4:1–15.

3537 *physiognomic science*: The art or pseudo-science of judging a person's character from their physical features, much practised in Goethe's day.

At the Well

3569 *In her shift in church*: Church and community joined in punishing and humiliating the woman who transgressed. See also 3575–6, 4436 and 4583; and the hateful incarnation of such attitudes in Valentin. As privy counsellor, Goethe supported the abolition of public penance in the Duchy of Weimar in 1786 and the retention of the death penalty for infanticide.

Shrine in the Town Wall

3586 SD *Mater Dolorosa*: Gretchen prays at an image of the Virgin Mary suffering (after Luke 2:35) at the foot of the Cross. Gretchen's verses recall the *Stabat Mater Dolorosa*, a thirteenth-century Latin hymn attributed to Giacopone da Todi.

Night

This scene, sketched in *Urfaust*, was not completed and integrated until 1806. Lines 3661–3, for example, were added to anticipate the by then completed 'Walpurgis Night'.

3669 *lion dollar*: 'A Dutch coin bearing the figure of a lion' (*OED*). As at 2675–6 Mephisto has the power to detect and raise buried treasure.

3682–97 *Sweet Kathrinchen . . . wear his ring*: A free and ironically moralistic adaptation of Ophelia's St Valentine's Day song in *Hamlet*, IV.5.48–63.

3698 *rat-catcher*: In *Romeo and Juliet*, III.1.72, Mercutio challenges

Tybalt with the words 'Tybalt, you rat-catcher, will you walk?'
There are some points of association between that play and *Faust*.
The Pied Piper of Hamelin also comes to mind, Faust and Mephisto
luring Gretchen away. Goethe published a poem on the Piper in
1803.

3715 *a capital offence is problematic*: Capital offences were dealt with
by courts claiming God's authority. Mephisto cannot intervene
there.

Cathedral

In *Urfaust* 'Cathedral' came immediately before, not after, 'Night', and
the requiem was stated to be for Gretchen's mother. *Faust. A Fragment*
finished with 'Cathedral'. In the final ordering of the scenes the deaths
of both the mother and the brother are alluded to (3787–9), as is also
Gretchen's pregnancy (3790–91). So her guilt and worry are com-
pounded on an occasion now dramatically less specific.

3798–3833 The Choir sings and the Evil Spirit paraphrases verses from
the *Dies Irae* sequence in the Mass for the Dead. The Latin means
'Day of wrath, that day/ Will dissolve the world into cinders . . .
(3798–9); 'Thus when the judge holds court,/ Whatever is hidden
will appear,/ Nothing will remain unavenged' (3813–15); 'What
then, wretch that I am, shall I say?/ Whom shall I appeal to for
advocate/ When even the just man is scarcely secure?' (3825–7).
There is a source in 1 Corinthians 15:52.

Walpurgis Night

St Walpurgis or Walburga, born in England, was abbess of Heidenheim
and died in 779. She was invoked against witchcraft. Her feast is 1 May.
In the night before, the witches celebrated their sabbath on the Brocken
in the Harz Mountains. Schierke and Elend are villages in the vicinity.
Goethe climbed the mountain in 1777 and was in the Harz again in
1783 and 1784. In the traditional Faust material there is no connection
between Faust and Walpurgis Night on the Brocken. It was first made
by a local comic author, Johann Friedrich Löwen, in his *Die Walpurgis-
Nacht* of 1756. Goethe, knowing that work or not, established the
connection seriously and for all time. Other mentions (at 2113, 2590
and in 'Black Day') seem to indicate that he intended it at the *Fragment*
or even the *Urfaust* stage; but he did not write the scene until the third
phase of work (chiefly 1799–1801). Among Goethe's many sources are
a work on witchcraft by Praetorius and a large engraving of a painting
by Michael Herr (1620) which depicts the Walpurgis Night revels.

3879–80 *rocks . . . blowing*: Two rocks along the way were known as the Snorers, because of the sound the wind made blowing through them.

3914–15 *we see ... Mammon inside the mountain*: A hyperbolic instance of the buried hoards that Mephisto is skilled at discovering. The Harz Mountains are famously rich in precious metals. Mammon himself appears in Matthew 6:24 ('Ye cannot serve God and mammon') and in *Paradise Lost*, Book I (building Satan the city of Pandemonium) as the personification of the evil of material wealth.

3962 *Mother Baubo*: In Greek mythology the lewd nurse who attempts to cheer up Demeter grieving for her lost daughter, Persephone. In Berlin there is a terracotta of her riding on a pig. Here she appears as a representative of the Ancient Greek world that Faust will enter in *Part II*. She joins several female figures on the Brocken in an ethos opposed to (male) Enlightenment rationality.

3964 *Honour ... due*: Alludes to Romans 13:7: 'Render therefore to all their dues: tribute to whom tribute is due; custom to whom custom; fear to whom fear; honour to whom honour.'

3968 *Ilsenstein*: North-east of the Brocken.

3974 *The way is wide*: Alludes (as does also line 52) to Matthew 7:13: 'Enter ye in at the strait gate: for wide is the gate, and broad is the way, that leadeth to destruction . . .'

3976–7 *Poke ... the womb*: Violent abortions, perhaps to be connected with line 4008. Witches were said to smear themselves and their broomsticks with an efficacious salve made from the fat of unborn babies.

4076–91 With these four characters, who take a quatrain each, Goethe broaches this scene's contemporary-satirical strain.

4119 *Lilith ... Adam's first wife*: Because there are two creation myths in Genesis – 1:27 and 2:18 ff. – rabbinical tradition supposed that Adam must have had a wife before he had Eve, and called her Lilith. Her name, or the word, occurs only once in the Bible, in Isaiah 34:14, where it has been taken to mean screech owl or night hag. She was the first refuser – she refused to lie under the dust of Adam – and by male priests fearing and hating women she was thoroughly demonized.

4129–35 *apple tree ... Apples ...* : Such imagery is found in the Song of Solomon (2:3, 2:5, 7:8) and in the Genesis account of the Fall (3:1–7).

4138–9, 4142–3 Indecencies (as also in 3961), explicit in Goethe's manuscript (and translated here), have usually been replaced by dashes in editions since 1808.

4144 *PROCTOPHANTASMIST*: A word coined from the Greek πρωτός (anus) and ψάντασμα (apparition). Coleridge (Table Talk, 6 January 1823) used the word 'phantasmist' to mean a person who maintains something to be a phantasm. And *Mist* in German means dung. The butt of the satire here is Friedrich Nicolai, who had written a parody of Goethe's *Werther* and remained his enemy thereafter. Nicolai, an arch-rationalist, was plagued around 1791 by hauntings and hallucinations, which he cured by applying leeches to his backside (see 4174), and lectured to the Berlin Academy on the experience. He was also a voluminous travel-writer (4169), and the victim of a practical joke (involving ghosts) at a house in Tegel (4161). This whole passage, sweet to Goethe no doubt and amusing to his readers, has, like much else in the scene, little or nothing to do with Faust.

4182 *mouse . . . red not grey*: The witch's soul would show itself as a grey mouse if she were dead. Traditionally, it shows as a red mouse if she is sleeping; here the red perhaps suggests, for her and Faust, a sort of waking dream.

4183–4208 These lines wrench the play (briefly) back to what matters in a vision akin to Coleridge's 'Night-mare Life-in-Death . . ./ Who thicks man's blood with cold' (*The Ancient Mariner*, Part III). By 'idol' (4190), I mean, as Goethe did, a phantom. Shelley translated the line: 'It is an enchanted phantom, a lifeless idol.'

4194 *the Medusa*: In Greek mythology she was one of three monstrous sisters (the Gorgons) whose gaze turned all who looked on them to stone.

4208 *Perseus*: A hero in Greek mythology. Looking only on the image of Medusa reflected in his shield, he cut off her head with a sickle.

4209–22 These lines were added late, to effect a transition into the Intermezzo.

4211 *the Prater*: The famous amusement park in Vienna, opened in 1766.

4214 *SERVIBILIS*: The name suggests an obsequious readiness to serve.

Walpurgis Night's Dream

About half the satirical quatrains making up this Intermezzo were written in 1797, two or three years before the 'Walpurgis Night' scene itself and having no connection with *Faust*. Goethe intended them as a sequel to the literary polemics he and Schiller had been conducting in their *Xenia* (a Greek word meaning 'friendly gifts'); and when Schiller demurred, Goethe dumped them, doubled in number, in *Faust*. (He used *Wilhelm Meister* and *Elective Affinities* similarly: as hold-alls for left-overs.) The epigrams, just about attached to the scene by passing references to witches, devils and unruly music and dancing, have no bearing on Mephisto, Faust and Gretchen, whose hastening tragic story they merely interrupt. Nor does the Intermezzo, despite its title and occasional characters, have anything substantive to do with Shakespeare's *A Midsummer Night's Dream* or *The Tempest*. And as polemic its force is by now very faint, the objects of the satire, many very unimportant even at the time, having long since gone into an obscurity from which only scholarship can, if it must and then not entirely, recover them.

4224 *Mieding*: John Martin Mieding, a cabinet-maker, was stage-manager and general factotum at the Weimar Court Theatre. Goethe commemorated him in a poem when he died in 1782.

4303 XENIA: These are the satirical epigrams mentioned above. Lines 4307–14 refer to August von Hennings, one of their targets. He had recently published an anthology called *Der Musaget* ('Leader of the Muses').

4318 *Parnassus*: A mountain in Greece, behind Delphi, closely associated with Apollo and the Muses. Thus 'Germany's Parnassus' means the canon or company of Germany's poets.

4323 CRANE: Goethe, in conversation with Eckermann (17 February 1829), identified the crane as the Swiss theologian Johann Caspar Lavater, with whom he had once been friendly. In the following quatrain the 'Worldling' is Goethe himself. He had appeared under that name in an early poem 'Diner zu Koblenz', seated between Lavater and J. B. Basedow, two of a kind. The Curious Traveller asking who the Crane is may be Nicolai (in 4267 ff. also).

4342 *As Orpheus did the brutes*: Orpheus' music had the power to gather the animals around him, listening. This quatrain and the one before it were added in 1826.

4343–62 Five quatrains parody various intellectual and philosophical positions before and after Kant.

4367–86 Five quatrains satirize various plights and behaviour, particularly among the émigrés, after the French Revolution. Sanssouci was the palace built for Frederick the Great at Potsdam. The name means 'without a care'. The Heavyweights may be the masses, empowered by the Revolution; or what Goethe elsewhere calls the 'literary *sans-culottes*'.

4395–8 Goethe intended to conclude his 'Walpurgis Night' very differently, not at all *pianissimo*. He made extensive notes for a climactic Satanic Mass, and completed about 150 lines of it in verse. These jottings set the scene: '*After the Intermezzo/ solitude, wilderness/*

*trumpets sound/ lightning, thunder from above./ Pillars of fire,
smoke, fog./ A rock towering up out of it./ It is Satan./ A multitude
all around./ A shortcoming/ how to force a way through./ Injury./
Shouting/ song./ They stand in the closest circle./ The heat is almost
unbearable./ Who stands closest in the circle./ Satan's speech etc./
Presentations./ Investitures.*' Satan makes a speech in praise of sex
and gold; Mephisto explains to a young girl, distressed because
she has not understood, how she may be enlightened; a vassal does
homage to Satan in a traditionally obscene way. Then should have
come a terrifying reprise and termination of the vision of Gretchen
(4183 ff.) from which Mephisto had drawn Faust away. A place
of execution appears. A chorus sings of killing and the spilling of
blood. The rest is notes: '*Press of people/ They climb a tree/ G./
Talk among the people/ On redhot ground/ The idol naked/ Hands
behind her back/ Neither her face nor her sex covered/ Singing/
Her head falls off/ Blood spurts forth and extinguishes the fire/
Night./ A rushing noise/ Hobgoblin-children chattering/ From
which Faust learns that . . .*' G. is Gretchen. For her apparition the
word 'idol' is used again. Unlike the Intermezzo, this projected
scene is funny, deadly serious and relevant. It would have led
directly into the *Urfaust* scene 'Black Day. Field' that follows.

Black Day. Field

Faust. A Fragment ended with the scene in the cathedral. 'Black Day',
'Night' and 'Prison', *Urfaust* material, were then all in prose, in which
state Goethe would not publish them. When he returned to them in
1798 he versified and expanded 'Prison'; left 'Night. Open Field' as it
was – in a prose so rhythmical and assonating that it could count as
verse; and let 'Black Day. Field' stand, as the only true prose, surviving
out of the earliest stratum of composition. Line-numbering, not used for
'Black Day', resumes with 'Night'.

[notes to pp. 158–60]

She's not the first: An observation made at the trial of Susanna
Margaretha Brandt (see Introduction, p. xxxii).

Dog! . . . monster! – O infinite Spirit: Faust must here be addressing the
Earth Spirit – but in a conception of him (having control over Mephisto,
knowing Faust's heart and soul) that belongs to a very early phase of
work on the play. Mephisto's cavorting in dog-shape (not just appearing
as a poodle) is likewise archaic and superseded, but survives.

Is all power . . . in earth: Matthew 28:18: 'And Jesus came and spake
unto them, saying, All power is given unto me in heaven and in earth.'

Night. Open Field

4399 *the Raven Stone*: A place of execution, outside town, where the unburied bodies would be left as carrion. The witches in *Macbeth* will come to mind, also the eerie night-ride in Gottfried August Bürger's ballad *Lenore* (1774).

Prison

4412–20 Like Ophelia, Gretchen – distracted – chants 'snatches of old tunes' (*Hamlet*, IV.7.176). This one comes from 'The Juniper Tree'. In that story, known to Goethe in an oral version and later collected by the brothers Grimm, a little boy is beheaded by his stepmother; is served up to and unwittingly eaten by his father; his sister buries his bones under a juniper tree, whereupon he turns into a bird and flies away singing. Gretchen's song is a version of the bird's; 'whore' and 'rogue' are her particular additions. Rightly she sees herself in tales and ballads. She did so when she sang 'There was a king in Thule . . .' and does so again in this scene at 4448–50.

4461 *the voice of my beloved friend*: Song of Solomon 2:8: 'The voice of my beloved! behold, he cometh leaping upon the mountains . . .' This takes up an earlier allusion (at 4435) to Song of Solomon 5:6: 'I opened to my beloved; but my beloved had withdrawn himself, and was gone . . .'

4511–14 *your hand . . . Blood on it*: From the murder of Valentin; blood as with Lady Macbeth in *Macbeth*, V.1.

4590 *the bell . . . white wand*: The bell is the *Armesünderglöcklein*, the 'poor sinner's bell', that tolled on the way to execution. A white wand was broken over the victim, before the beheading.

4596 *Why was I born? I curse the day!*: Alludes to Job 3:3: 'Let the day perish wherein I was born.'

4609 *Encamp around*: Alludes to Psalms 34:7: 'The angel of the Lord encampeth round about them that fear him, and delivereth them.'

4611 *saved*: In *Urfaust* there is no suggestion that Gretchen is 'saved'.